# The Golden Star of Halich

*Eric P. Kelly*

BOOKS ABOUT POLAND

By Eric Kelly

———

The Trumpeter of Krakow
The Blacksmith of Vilno
The Golden Star of Halich

*The Burning of Krylos*

(Border from patterns in Ruthenian Museum Lvov.)

# The Golden Star of Halich

## A TALE OF THE
## RED LAND IN 1362

BY ERIC P. KELLY

*Illustrated by Angela Pruszynska*

NEW YORK : THE MACMILLAN COMPANY : 1931

SET UP AND ELECTROTYPED BY THE J. S. CUSHING CO.
PRINTED BY THE BERWICK & SMITH CO.

This Book is Dedicated

TO

MARY ELLEN MERRILL

So fleet the works of men back to the Earth again:
Ancient and Holy things fade like a dream.

CHARLES KINGSLEY

# CONTENTS

# CONTENTS

# ILLUSTRATIONS

*Halich in the Twelfth Century*
(Ornament from Church of St. Stanislaus,
formerly Tserkiev St. Pantalemon.)

# Prologue

# There Was a City

THERE was a city, the name of it Halich; and it lay upon
the bosom of the East where it turns to meet the West.
And men thought it the fairest city that the eastern lands
had known. For about it wound the mighty river which the
Greeks called Tyras and the Slavs Dniester, and near it grew

[ xiii ]

great forests that shut Heaven from the sight of man with their lofty branches, and on its hills rose castles and churches and palaces, and in the gray distance the lofty Carpathians swung gently to the south. The armies that marched up to its gates or thronged its streets were clad in armor that shone with silver and gold; the white-sailed vessels that sped upstream from the Black Sea and the port of Byzantium carried cargoes of spices and silks and diamonds and rubies. In its streets went the men of Rus, the men of Hungary, the men of Poland; with them were merchants and men of trade from Armenia, Germany, Byzantium. Indeed the Mongol, the Avar, and the Tartar were as much at home here as in the Orient, and over all this life lay the languid spell of the East.

But despite this spell, there was ever the busy hum of men in Halich. The city lay upon the road from Byzantium to the Baltic, the road from Kiev and Vladimir to Lechia, the road from the Volga and Dnieper to Hungary through the Carpathian Mountains. Salt mines were worked in the neighboring hills and many a monarch of the East paid a high stipend for salt. Ships loaded with it went down the Dniester to the Black Sea, past the city of Tyras or Olesia which the Tartars named Akkerman. There ran through this city the great north and south highway from Greece and Wallachia and the Eastern Roman Empire, by which the caravans traveled to the Baltic and the great cities to the north; this route was very ancient, one of the three "Szlaks" (trails) by which Asia poured into Europe. Along these routes, cities and states and even civilizations had perished, for not only merchants but armies of invaders passed over them; the wild steppe had borne red flowers of fire and blood, and devastation and destruction had reared their heads everywhere.

Now when this city of Halich was in its prime it was the heart that gave blood to all the Slav lands. He who was ruler here was grand duke of all the lands of Rus, and held as tributary to himself the dwellers in Trembovla, Zvinogrod, Kiev, and even distant Suzdal. He ruled in his castle on Krylos Hill where rose the dome of the Cathedral and the palace; and the city at his feet, extending clear to the banks of the Dniester and bounded by the Tchev and Lukva Rivers, was seven miles long and four miles broad. Princes of the Eastern Roman Empire flattered him and sought his hand in marriage for their daughters and sent him jewels in the flitting boats that sailed up the Dniester past the rapids at Yampol. And all the boyars (warriors of noble blood) that were his subjects, and the princes and heroes of his druzina (ducal following), and the merchants who bowed before him, and the peasants who lived on the flat lands and were called "smerd" or stinking ones—all these believed that such splendor had always been and would always be. Into the blue sky of his city rose the domes and spires of more than a hundred tserkievs and churches—through its streets went the roar of trade—and up and down the lands along the river rose the songs of peasants who lived from harvest to harvest and knew that God would bring all things.

But all things come to an end and so was it with Halich, for out of the East there came the Tartar hordes to overrun the lands of Rus and Poland and Hungary. Bravely the men of Halich set out against them and they landed men and beasts upon the bank of the river Kalka. But the Tartars fell upon them with the fury of wild beasts, rode them down with lines of cavalry that extended beyond the horizons, and threw their horses into a panic by hurling among them round substances that burned fiercely with a roar and a burst of smoke, and tore men's bodies apart. Panic reigned upon the border lands for seventeen years, and the divided Slavs were once more drawn together to withstand the invader from Asia. It was of no avail however, for in the year 1241 the Tartars stood before Halich, having come upon it from the north. Behind them the Russian and Polish lands were but a smoking ruin. Kiev with its hundred towers lay in ashes— Vladimir, Belz, Chelm, and Zvinogrod held not a living soul. Batu-Khan, the Tartar leader, having taken all the cities of the border save Krzemienca, was angered at the opposition he had found there, and swore to put all Halich to the sword. About Halich for days and days swarmed the armies of the Horde, the carts creaked, the camels brayed, the horses filled the air with such a screaming that every voice vanished in its presence. The men of Halich defended themselves valiantly but they were like to a grasshopper upon which huge ants have fallen. They perished to a man and their bodies filled houses, streets, and shrines, poisoning the air. Batu-Khan destroyed the walls, plundered the buildings, assured himself that not one living thing remained in Halich. Then he marched to the south.

# CHAPTER I

## A DAGGER MISSES ITS MARK

THE sun was aslant in the late afternoon across the city of Lvov, which the Poles designated as Lwow, the Germans Lemberg, and the French and Greeks Leopol. It was August, the Month of the Sickle, 1362. And in the golden weather there went up to the skies the sound of hammering, the crashing of building-stones, and the hewing of beams. For it was the reign of Kazimir, whom men of that day called King of the Peasants but later generations the Great, and it was he who rebuilded the Polish nation, beginning with the West and ending in the Red Land of the East, the capital of which was Lvov. Beneath his hands Krakow had grown from a ducal fortress to a medieval capital city, and with this finished he had turned to Lvov where there had been but a provincial grod, or town, located with a castle on a hill, weakly fortified with wooden walls, and open to assault after assault from the East. After bitter wars with the Lithuanian and Tartar this city lay a veritable heap of ruins, but with the coming of Kazimir it suddenly leaped to life. It was he who moved it from its clustering circle at the base of the Zamek Hill: he made of it a walled town with the hill and the river as its defences. He laid out a square plot of land somewhat to the right of the old town, and there with his architects designed a city of the best medieval type, with its walls and defences, and upper and lower castles, a cathedral, and many churches for Pole, Armenian, Wallachian, Greek, and Rus.

# THE GOLDEN STAR OF HALICH

But the lengthened shadows had not brought cessation of labors to the builders in Lvov: they were working for their own safety and for the city's good, for who could tell but in that very night, perhaps, some prying Tartar tribe might fall upon the unfinished city and massacre all within it? Some men were building walls that ran along the little stream, the Peltev; others were at work upon bastions at the gates adjoining the new Rynek or market place. Some were at work upon the new residential palace at the extreme left of the market where the walls from south and west met, and others were at work upon an upper castle to be used chiefly for defence and military purposes.

And among the workers went scores of tradesmen and merchants from other lands to complete sales, purchases, and exchanges; there were Armenians in their yellow robes, fezzed and turbaned Turks at whom men looked askance, Wallachians in their braided jackets, Karaites or "Saracens" from the south who wore garments of only one material, all wool or all linen or all haircloth; Tsigani, the Asiatic gypsy folk who had left the cities of India behind them, and in colored garments bedecked with ribbons went from place to place living by their wits, the women selling charms, and the men horses to such as would buy; Greeks in dark robes with silver trimmings, a few masked women in embroidered robes, well protected by retinues of giant men; Polish women riding jauntily on horseback, unveiled and in pleasant contrast to their Eastern sisters; warriors from Lithuania, Suzdal, and even Moskva—East and West mingling in barter and trade, or even meeting in friendship, or dispute, for a law court had been set up by order of the king, and justice was now open to the humblest peasant.

But suddenly among all these in the market and among the soldiers that stood by the Krakow Gate, there was evident a strange uneasiness, an uneasiness growing to restlessness and fast rushing to excitement; the watchman high up over the portal had long been watching a cloud of dust that rose in the air along the route that ran to Przymysl, Tarnov, and Krakow. Now, as figures began to emerge from it and outline themselves against it —"Horsemen," the guard was shouting—"on the Krakow road" —and following his words came the commands of officers and the rushing to arms of the soldiers. But as the riders came nearer the reassuring words "Polish cavalry" fell from the lips of the guard to the ears of the anxious ones below. Anxious no longer, though still swept with excitement, the soldiers pressed forward toward the entrance to the city and the crowd in the market came dashing behind them. "Riders, from Krakow," went up the cry on every side; above, casements were thrown open; below, men, women, and children dashed forward to see the spectacle; the beggars left the church doors to hurry to a source of new gain, the peasants forgot their wares spread about on the ground—all was hurry and confusion.

And now all could hear the beat of hoofs upon the road, all could see the dust and the reflection cast by the sun upon the arms and livery of the men on horseback. They were coming along the road at a full gallop as if not yet confident that they would reach the city before nightfall, and it was well known by travelers in this turbulent Eastern province that stout city walls were none too great a protection in the midst of such foes as lurked about in the darkness. And as they clattered through the gate amidst cheering and bowing and occasional flower-throwing, the curious onlookers could see that in the company were a dozen men and that one man riding ahead was of more spirited bearing than the rest, though he was indeed well upon middle age, as his thick body and the whitened hair sticking out from a leather helmet which well-nigh concealed his features evidenced.

At first glance one would think them all men of the country

nobility, men used to freedom, unhampered by the rules of court, courageous, as much at home upon horses as upon the soil of their estates, kindly in visage, stamped definitely with the seal of the West which writes men's character upon their faces and does not cloak it as does the East beneath a mask that may be expressionless, or, having expression, may serve as a mere counterfeit for the soul beneath.

They were dressed for the most part alike—thick leather jackets that were caught together at the front in braid and fell a little below the waist, while rising to the waist was a form of leather hose, lined with soft wool to keep the stiffness from the skin. At their belts they carried short swords. They were not arrayed for serious fighting; an attack of spearmen at close quarters would have been fatal to them all, but the leather they wore was stout enough to turn aside blows from staves or coarsely tempered pikes. Their main dependence, one could see, was upon speed, for they wore light clothes in order to ride lightly; and indeed if attacked by a party wearing heavy armor or even light chain they could easily outride them and escape. From the appearance of the horses' streaked and smoking flanks they had ridden far that day.

Near the edge of the crowd amidst a pile of beams that lay waiting the carpenters' tools for shaping into house supports, there stood on this afternoon two very strange-looking men watching the riders intently. Had it not been that Lvov was an Oriental city and held within its walls so many different types of men and women from West and East alike, the attention of the crowd might have been attracted to these two men. But in the motley company that ranged itself around the gates, these two were not so unlike many others—one might have taken them for mountebanks, Tartars perhaps, or Tsigani (gypsies). One of them was a dwarf, with a great hump upon his back, a long nose, small eyes, a smooth face, a ring in one ear—there was no other ear, which might have led the guard to suspect that he had once been caught at cheating and been deprived of that useful member with one stroke of a sharp knife; he wore a kirtle-like garment that fell from neck to knees, caught at the waist and open at the throat. The other, far from being a dwarf, was a giant in stature, though not a giant in girth, for he was as tall and as straight as a bean-pole. His forehead was high, eyes deep set, lips narrow and cruel, and a heavy yellow beard made the face seem wider than it really was. He wore a suit of black, head to foot, tight-fitting, embroidered with gold—black hose beneath an overfolding mantle, and long, narrow sandals. There was an air of precision about him that marked him at once as a man of superior station, and when he addressed the dwarf it was with a certain air of disdain—even contempt.

"Master Phokas—Master Phokas," the dwarf was saying.

"Call me not that, you fool," he whispered hotly. "Keep your tongue in your face or you will soon lose it."

The dwarf bowed but there was black trouble upon him and he could not restrain his speech. "How shall I know which is he? There are more than a dozen of them."

"You need not know him," the other retorted. "Keep your eye upon me, and let your aim be swift and accurate when I nod my head. They are coming this way now. Stand ready!"

The tall man glanced behind them at a small dark lane that lost itself amidst wooden buildings, as if assuring himself of a quick retreat.

Just as he turned around, a whole band of boys who had been playing at quarter-staff in a neighboring court came rushing up to the crowd with shouts of excitement and keen pleasure.

"Michael," shouted one, "I think these be szlachta (nobles) from Krakow."

"No," exclaimed another, panting and with red cheeks, "these are merchants from Tarnov."

"Merchants not at all," Michael shouted the words. "See how they ride. See how they sit on their horses. These men are knights. . . . Vivat. . . . Vivat . . ."

"Greeting," shouted a horseman in return, for the retinue was just opposite them now, and the rider waved a hand to the boys over the heads of the crowd; Michael, catching the salute, leaped upon a pile of beams and waved his hat in the air.

"Which is he, Master Phokas?" sounded a sharp voice at his elbow.

And then, in a flash, the face of the whole world altered, for up from behind the beams, so close that the boy could reach out and touch them, rose two men, a tall man and a dwarf of no stature at all. The tall man pointed at the leader of the horseman, his arm straight as an arrow, and in a space so brief that one's heart had scarce time to beat twice, there quivered in the right hand of the dwarf a short blade, a dagger blade that was sharp with the finest edge. The last ray of the sun fell upon it and turned its steel to blood, as back it shot toward the dwarf's shoulder as the muscles tensed his arm ready for the throw; but just as the arm suddenly slipped its tension, like a bow-string springing back as the arrow is discharged—at that instant a boy leaped from the pile of beams directly upon the dwarf. That one swerved to avoid the blow, swerved but an inch perhaps, but by that inch and the deflection it brought, the soul remained within the body of the horseman, across whose very eyes flew the streak of steel like a lightning flash.

"I have him!" a boy's cry rang out, but in the next instant he was flung upon the ground as the tall man followed by the dwarf leaped across the market and disappeared in the dark lane between the buildings. "What? what?" was the cry of wonder that went

*The Attempted Assassination*

(Detail includes portal of Armenian Cathedral, Lvov, and lower border is
Byzantine-Russian-Ruthenian)

up from the crowd—"An assassin?"   "Catch him!" and a whirling tumult arose round the spot.   And as Michael, somewhat stunned, rose confusedly to his feet, horsemen who had followed the leader rode through the crowd toward the lane, their short swords out of their belts.   "Assassins!"   "Stop them!" came the cry from all about.

But one might better have tried to stop the wind, for in the millionth of a second that had followed the dagger's flight the men had utterly vanished.   And though the troops came down from the Krakow gate, and the peasants and the horsemen searched the dark lane from end to end, it was a search utterly without result.   The assailants had evidently planned their escape perfectly—and their attack too, for that matter, had not a mere chance upset their plans.   So that when the horsemen, returning to their leader who awaited them, espied Michael who had followed them to the head of the lane, they took him along with them.

"It was this boy," said one to the leader, "who leaped upon one of the men who attacked you."

"I had not been alive, else," exclaimed the other.   "That knife missed my temple by a mere hair's breadth.   What is your name, boy?"

"Michael Korzets."   His heart was beating hard now.

"Korzets," the leader shouted, turning his head.   One of the riders, who had been delayed for a few minutes by business with the guard at the gate, dashed forward from the rear of the band where the attack on the leader had just been made known to him. His eyes no sooner fell upon Michael and Michael's upon him, than they were in each other's arms.

"Father," said the boy, trembling with emotion, for now that the incident was over he felt suddenly weak, "I thought you were in Krakow."

[ 9 ]

"I was. But that comes later. Did you see the attempt upon this man's life?"

The leader waved his right hand as if to interpose. "He saved my life. Had he not sprung upon the thrower I would be lying in state to-morrow. . . . A desperate deed too," he muttered to himself, "here in the market place in the midst of all these people. Who can have known?"

Upon the father's face had come a pride that was good to look upon. "This is a happy hour for the name of Korzets," he said softly in the boy's ear, then stood silently as if awaiting commands from the leader.

"Go mount your horse and lead us to your house," said that one at length. "Let four of you remain here to help the soldiers scour this town for traces of the two men. I doubt if you will find even traces."

Korzets ran for his horse and swung Michael up in front of him, and the whole company galloped after him across the market to the town houses of the country nobility on the farther side. The journey was short and swift, but it gave Michael time to ponder upon a few questions that had assailed him since he first saw his father. What could be the meaning of all this? Why had his father returned from Krakow where he had gone some-days previous at summons from the Crown? Why had he returned without his usual retinue, in this ordinary attire without family crest or distinguishing mark to set him apart from the crowd? Who could the other horsemen be, and who could the leader be—the leader with a visage that seemed somehow familiar, the deep lines of care upon it, the noble forehead, the beard turning gray?

The ugly face of the dwarf came upon him suddenly in his thoughts and he shuddered; what could he be—a dweller in the eastern or southern lands? And why this attempt upon the life of a nobleman, for so the leader's bearing stamped him, in the very heart of a populous town? And that other being, the tall man in black—he with something of the Bulgar about him? The skill with which the act itself had been executed had no wonder in it for him, for he knew that there were many men practised deeply in this art of hurling a knife, some who could send a blade with deadly accuracy into a living heart.

It was already dusk when they reached the Korzets house at the eastern extremity of the town; upon the Rynek, fires were glowing where the merchants were cooking their evening meal —the watchmen were lighting their torches in the merchants' fires, and the sound of songs and prayers rose softly in the air. Above their heads in the sky, light-blue in the last afterglow, the uneven outlines of the new and unfinished buildings rose proudly. What a city this was to be, Michael thought—this city upon the eastern border of Poland. For in the past there had been nothing but bloodshed—here no man's life was safe, no race of people might dwell without constant fear of extinction. It had been first the prey of roving and quarrelsome boyars, then of the wild tribes of the steppe, then of the Tartars whose depredations were far greater than those of any of the others. Poles had lived in these lands since the beginning of time—yet until this day there had been no cessation of bloodshed, famine, and slaughter. In old days the capital city had been Halich, the magnificent grod of the old boyars of Rus, but that capital had been destroyed many times, and although rebuilt in part was but the shadow of its former glory. This city was to be a new capital of the Red Lands—this Lvov was the city of the Lion, the city of King Kazimir.

In the old days Lev, the grandson of Danilo of Halich, had built his castle on the high hill above the market. About this grew up the ducal grod with its churches and tserkievs (churches of the Greek rite) and market place. But when the family of Lev had come to an end or had departed from the Red Land, then Kazimir, King of Poland, had placed this whole land beneath his protection. He had changed the grod to a walled town—the work upon the fortifications was going forward even now; he would make of this city an outpost of western civilization; here might man stand and hold the East in defiance.

When they reached the house, the horses were led away by servants, and the greatest excitement reigned at the unexpected return of the master and his guests.

The house was the typical dwelling of a border noble, and though lacking the broad acres which the dwor or country place possessed yet it boasted a small orchard, a garden, and a spacious courtyard. It was two stories high, built of wood with stone foundation, and round the court and orchard land ran a strong palisade wall of rough logs which offered defence against small bodies of men should they by any chance penetrate through the guards at the city walls. In the courtyard was the well, around it the buildings which housed the servants and the horses; the women servants, if not married, slept for the most part in the immense kitchen, while the women of the family slept in the second story of the house, to which they ascended by a ladder-like staircase.

Amidst the turmoil caused by the arrival of the guests, the greeting by the women, the running for water, the grooming of horses, the scurrying about for fuel, and the slicing of huge quarters of beef to be roasted over open fires, could be heard the happy voices of the women of the family greeting the home-comers, and the questioning by the stay-at-homes of the knights from Krakow. What was going on in the capital? What were women wearing? Were those tall, pointed hats with dangling ribbons still in favor? Were falcons' wings dyed this season? And what was the favorite color at court? Pieces of family silver plate were brought out and polished for the most honored of the guests:

the others must eat from plates of wood. When finally the meal was prepared and the servants in procession came bearing platter after platter of food, the leader was seated at the head of the table in the place of honor and before him burned two yellow tapers. Torches of pine knots thrust into sockets in the wall threw down a smoky light upon the rest of the company. To them all, Polish hospitality was extended lavishly, and above the door in carven letters were the words: "Gosc w domu, Bog w domu"—A guest in the house is God in the house.

At length the meal was at an end, and the honey mead had crowned the feast, and the benches were removed to the side of the room nearest the open casements, for it was a bit sultry and the air felt comforting upon the face. The leader however sat apart from the others in a high-backed chair, and motioned at the close of the meal for Michael to remain although his father had signaled to the boy to depart.

"He has earned the right to be present," he said; "this is his day for he has saved a life. In the proper place and at the proper time he may ask his reward; if it be reasonable and within my power to grant he shall have what he desires . . . Now . . . ," he addressed Michael's father, "you may tell him whose life he has saved."

Jan Korzets, father of the boy, took Michael's right hand in his own and approached the leader. When he had come close to him, he fell upon one knee and Michael did the same.

"It is your King."

Michael's eyes blazed: "Indeed I had guessed it, your majesty."

The King smiled gravely. Leaning forward he gazed into the boy's face. Michael was fifteen, lean, lanky, but with hard muscles like whip braids—his eyes and hair were brown; the King tweaked a lock of hair back from his forehead with a sudden motion of his arm, then leaning back smiled again, but the action said more to Michael than any number of words could express—his heart thumped for joy and a glow seemed to surround his whole body. But with this action the incident was closed. In another moment Kazimir was in low-voiced conversation with one of the knights.

"Bring the man here," he said.

And as Michael looked back upon this incident from a viewpoint of later years he realized that with these words of the King there came upon him a kind of spell. It was somehow the opening of the gates to a new world, and besides that, it seemed as if magic were at work. It was not merely the beginning of a new adventure—it was more like the entrance into a land of mystery, of strange happenings.

"Bar the doors and windows," the King commanded, "and be sure that there are guards at gate and casement."

Jan Korzets himself executed this command.

The torches were burning low, filling the room with a pitchy smell—the air was smoky and close.

A young man came forward, knelt before the King, and then arose to his feet.

"You have been to Halich?"

"I am just returned."

"What did you see there?"

"Strange actions, your majesty. Something is going forward there that I could not fathom. I was in the new town and saw the bishop. He told me that the peasants everywhere about are in terror, that the forests are full of strange warriors and Tartars."

"Did you hear any reports of what is going on in the old city?"

"Yes." The smoke in the air made the scene one of unreality to Michael. The subdued tones of the questioner, the apparently excited voice of the spy, the quiet eagerness of the knights leaning forward—what mystery and conspiracy were here? "In the ruined city itself there is great building going on, particularly upon Krylos Hill where still stand the walls and towers of the old Cathedral and castle; one may hear the sound of hammers all night long."

"Did you see many men?"

"I saw many types of armed men, though no great armies; there are at most a few hundred there, but they come from many places."

"What languages did you hear?"

"Rus, Tartar, Lithuanian, some Polish, Bulgar, and a tongue that I knew not; it had a classic ring, perhaps Latin, perhaps Greek."

"Are there ships in the river?"

"There are, your majesty. Curious galleys below the city, drawn up in the shelter of the banks beyond that point where the Dniester curves to the south. They are small, with a single bank of rowers, and a wide sail that dips far on either side of the middle mast. The prows are high and rounding—from the sterns project wooden beams; each well-braced and knobbed, tipped with sharp steel like the head of a broad spear. The sails are black, and the three pennons are of purple."

"Purple?" The King started from his chair in excitement. "Are you sure?"

"I am. Imperial purple."

"What did you hear?"

The man glanced about fearfully. "Your majesty, I heard only fragments of talk, for there is some fearful secret there. The dwellers in the new portion of the city are afraid for their lives, but dare not flee lest the Tartars or some other tribe fall upon them in the night beyond the city."

At that the King rose to his feet and walked back and forth up and down the room. "Then tell me all you know," he broke out impatiently after a minute. "I hear rumors in Krakow that all is not well in Halich. I call a council of my knights and none of them know what is happening. I decide to come to Lvov to find out—I come here in the simple garb of a country gentleman —no one knows I have left Krakow—no one knows I am come here, and yet—" he turned to the circle of intent faces—"and yet an assassin meets me at the very gate of Lvov and hurls his dagger in my face. What then am I to do? The Lithuanian has promised me peace, the Tartar is still at Sarai and the Krim —who can it be that threatens me in my own kingdom—in Halich?"

"It is not one people—there are many peoples there," said the spy, "and," he lowered his voice and whispered, "and they all say that they are led there by the Golden Star."

"The *Golden Star?*"

"Yes—it is what they say—the Golden Star of Halich."

Each man looked at his neighbor. Jan Korzets demanded: "What do you think the Golden Star means?"

"I don't know. . . . I don't know, your majesty," repeated the spy as the King's eyes flamed upon him—"I can guess, but my guess is only as good as the guess of any. Perhaps the Golden Star is a great talisman, for I know that all the eastern nations believe in such symbols; it might be a decoration that is worn about the neck—it might be some piece upon the altar of church or tserkiev, it might be the handle of a sword, or the centerpiece of a crown. But it seems to me that it must be something to these people of the East such as the Holy Grail is to us in the West, or perhaps the sword of Charlemagne or the horn of Roland. There is a sacred spear in the treasury of the Mongols at Sarai, and in the name of this spear millions of men in Asia would take arms and gladly die in battle."

"What think you?" The King addressed Jan Korzets.

# A DAGGER MISSES ITS MARK

"I have no thoughts—though perhaps the Golden Star might be a sign in the Heavens. The Greek astrologers tell us that man's life is governed by the stars, and perhaps the Golden Star is some sign that will appear in the sky."

The King asked: "What star now dominates the Heavens?"

One of the company who delved into astrology answered: "The sun is now in the house of Leo. Regulus is the great star of that constellation though it doth not now appear in the sky. The sun itself is the dominating star of the house."

"Regulus—it means nothing," replied the King, "but Leo—that is the house of the Lion, and the lion is the symbol of this city and of the house of Lev. Can it be? Can it be? . . . No. . . .

"But"—and he was tense with the power of his words, "this is what I came here to learn. It is evident that there is some conspiracy against me in the Red Lands—in Halich. Yet in all these centuries there has been in these lands nothing but bloodshed and slaughter. Cities have been destroyed and human life has not been worth the straw that flies before the wind. What do I do? I come back here to the land of the ancient Lechs, the land from which our people have been driven in terror. I restore their homes to them, I build castles and walls and ramparts. I set up courts and churches and schools. The East shall no longer dominate these lands. They belong to the West. This is no mere Tartar raid—this is no Lithuanian foray—this is something more subtle—what then can this mean, this talk of a Golden Star?"

Back and forth, up and down the room he strode while the others waited breathless. Then turning upon Jan Korzets with terrific suddenness he gave commands with a fury like that of hail when it bursts forth from a cloud.

"Go for me to Halich. Get at the bottom of all this. Find out what men are plotting against me there and why they seek my life. I tell you that there are forces in Halich which no king dare slight. And yet the time is not ripe for me to move there with an army. It might spoil all. It might be just what my enemies wished. Find out for me why men talk of the Golden Star, and find out what this Golden Star is. No," and one of those impulses that came ever upon him suddenly, leaped into his brain "—bring me this Golden Star. If you count yourself of valor and wish to show yourself zealous in the support of your King, bring me this trophy—if trophy it be. For if it is an emblem for my crown, then my crown will shine with more luster and power, and if it is something for the Church, then bring it, in God's name, from those who know not its value. I would have this thing, this Golden Star. I would possess it."

The eagerness upon his face was almost a spasm. The commands came flowing like the waters of a down-rushing brook and the words themselves were fiery and pointed. Jan Korzets fell upon one knee before him and put his lips to the signet ring on his hand: "I will bring you the Golden Star," he swore, "though I go to the end of the earth."

But suddenly another voice, shrill, keen, alive with feeling sprang into the air: "And I will go. It is the favor that you have promised."

They turned to Michael in surprise, for he, seemingly forgetful of his position, had stepped forward into the circle before the King. But suddenly realizing that he had thrust himself forward among his elders, men noble and of reputation, he felt a quick burst of shame; yet he had no need for the blush that colored his cheeks when the King sensed the fervor that lay behind the words.

"The words of a man. You may go."

And Michael, ready to sob for joy, for pride, for love, for loyalty to this ruler and overlord, fell upon one knee before him again, and remained there until his father led him away.

# CHAPTER II

## THE TSIGAN RAFT

AT a very early hour the next morning, a company of a dozen men left Lvov and struck off into the meadows to the south in the direction of Halich. They were mounted upon horses of the steppe, not overlarge, but keen and full of fire and experienced in battle and chase. The riders were not laden with the heavy armor, however, which men carry into battle; instead they wore light chain links over leather jackets and carried swords; two had bows slung over their shoulders and one carried a heavy cross-bow.

Their leader was Jan Korzets. He was distinguished from his men only in that his apparel seemed brighter and of more costly workmanship, and that he wore a light cloth mantle over the chain links. At his side rode Michael, proudly in the stirrups of his first expedition, well versed by constant training in the lore of horsemanship, and no stranger to the thick leather outfit and the metal upon it. For a while the horses trod upon the hard pasture land, then passing by a clump of trees came to a trail that was well beaten down.

"The Roman road," said one.

"Not so," replied the elder Korzets. "This is the road of traders which runs from the Red Land to the land of the Wallachians, and branching near the Pruth goes east and south to the Krim. The Romans built their roads across the hills, not on the lowlands or in valleys where there might be ambush."

# THE GOLDEN STAR OF HALICH

The sun mounted, changed from red to yellow, the dew dried from the grass, and the songs of the birds became less frequent. Across the meadows, where the great steppe began and rolled to the east for hundreds of miles, steaming clouds of mist were arising, disclosing hundreds of birds and animals—foxes, rabbits, martins—storks perched upon one leg, field mice, and other scurrying things. Along this trail they traveled, had gone in ages past great races of mankind; it lay to the east of the circle where the Carpathians sweep to the south, and it ran from the watershed of northern Europe to the watershed of southern Europe. Across this trail men carried rude boats, when peoples were going by the rivers from the Black Sea to the Baltic or from the Danube to the far-circling Volga. Here was a space between the northflow and the southflow of the rivers and through it swung the Vandals, the Croats, the Goths, the Huns, and later the Avars. To the west the Carpathians, to the east the steppe, the long steppe where Asia gathered her forces to pour into Western Europe.

Amidst such traditions as these Michael's soul was exulting in romance. They were now upon the highway where adventure might raise its head at any moment. He had never been so far from the city in this territory before: their country house lay to the north of Lvov and their journeying had always been in that direction. This was the territory of ruins, tree-grown cellars and pits, mounds and crumbling walls; over this land had lain for centuries the hand of invasion and plunder. Once in the dim past there had been peace here when the Lechs, ancestors of the Poles, the Russini folk, and the Wallachians had lived here side by side—yes, even with the Hungarian and the Czech; but since the days of the wars among the boyars and the coming of the Tartars, no peasant dared build a hut within miles of this trail. Yet it was a fair land, and a rich land, and the black soil nourished crops that far outdid in number and richness the crops of any other section in Europe.

And as they went farther and the day grew warmer, and in the distance could be seen the hills that run from the Carpathians down to the Dniester, Michael felt more and more the grip of some powerful influence upon him, something like magic. For there is something about mystery that appeals most strongly to the young, and here was a boy sharing in a quest that might solve the mystery that had baffled a king. The men were taking every precaution not to be noticed, for the mission in itself was a secret one, and they knew that spies were abroad, after the incident of the knife-throwing in the city the day before. Therefore, at a command from the leader they turned aside from the trail when the hills began to appear, and rode on the hard, needle-strewn turf through the clearings in the light woods that bordered the trail.

By dusk the highlands that lay beyond the Dniester seemed very close; one could reach Halich by morning perhaps by spurring ahead along the trail, but Jan Korzets had his own plan, namely to approach the city quietly, and from a point above it on the river, instead of riding in by the bridge which connected the new town with the north bank. By a slow approach one could perhaps pick up information on the way, and could investigate the story that the woods about the city were full of armed men. At nightfall a halt was made, some hares shot during the day by the archers were brought in and roasted, and when it came sleeping time, four men remained constantly on guard.

Morning came without further adventure, and they were upon their way again, but as they neared the river, the leader decided to swing sharply upstream, keeping on their left the high hill which towered above the Dniester on the farther side. This hill was but one end of a high ridge that bordered Halich on the west, the city lying between two ridges, this and another, both of them rising above rivers; the west ridge rose above the River Tchev, and the east ridge above the River Lukva, which the Poles call Lukiev. The Dniester skirted the old city on the north side, but just beyond the lower ridge turned sharply to the south and skirted the east side. The bridge lay across the Dniester nearly three miles to the east from the point where Korzets' party emerged from the woods and turned upstream.

This then was Halich, the city of splendor and renown—the jewel of the Red Land in the old days. Michael, turning about on his horse's back, scanned the scene eagerly, but from this point there was little to see. A bare expanse of hill rising sharply—a sluggish stream flowing into the Dniester, marshes, pasture land, with here and there sheep—was there no trace of the magnificence of the old city? Yes, there were a building and a tower; the blood leaped into his heart. The tower was upon the hill just across the Dniester; it was flat-sided and not round like many of the eastern churches; that he could see, but there was no cross upon it.

"What is that?" he asked one of the older men.

The man looked for a long time. "I am not sure—I think it is the tower upon the Tserkiev (church of the Greek rite) of St. Pantalemon, though I am not sure."

"And it is in Halich?"

"Yes, though not in the grod (city). The grod lies about four miles beyond it."

Michael continued to look as they rode along.

They were close to the water now. Immediately under their eyes rolled the Dniester swollen by heavy rains. At several points they could see the marks of travel, the prints of horses' hoofs and men's footprints, approaching directly to the water's edge and disappearing as if they had forded the stream. Gazing at all of these Jan Korzets shook his head; the river seemed everywhere too high for crossing on this flat land; in olden times the old salt trails had been here and along them conquering armies had passed, but even in those days the fords were treacherous and on one occasion three hundred men had been engulfed by a sudden rise in the river.

"No crossing here," muttered the leader, at one place where they had halted briefly for refreshment. "The flood will not go down for weeks, perhaps not until freezing time."

"It may be possible, just above. See—the river widens just beyond the point where the forest touches the shore." It was one of the archers who made the suggestion.

"Go and see."

The man rode off quickly and disappeared in the thicket of trees. A few minutes later he emerged, smiling, and rode up to his leader.

"I have found something. Not a ford, but a raft."

"A raft?"

"Yes, and large enough for us all. A company of Tsigan folk making their way downstream have tied it there while they gather provisions. They will not use it themselves until nightfall."

Jan Korzets, Michael, and three of the men made their way along the shore to the forest edge at the place indicated by the archer. Then entering the clump of trees they rode slowly along until the Tsigan camp lay before them.

Seated upon the ground about a fire was a company of swarthy men and women in clothes of the greatest assortment of styles and colors that Michael had ever seen. Though these people were in rags and tatters yet they had wound their waists about with wide scarfs of brilliantly colored cloth; they wore gold rings in their ears, and there was much jewelry hanging about their necks. Yet many of them were barefoot and their lower garments were hanging in fringes. Over the fire was a pot hanging from three sticks, and stirring it as if her life depended on it was an old, toothless woman, as hideous and as ugly as she was old. Over toward the fire some young men were examining horses that had just been driven in, and in wagons beyond, one could hear the sound of laughter and singing, and amidst this noise rose the pleasant shouting of ragged children at play.

Suddenly someone began to sing, and in a second, the song was picked up from every corner of the camp; the words were in a curious old dialect, older even than the dialect of the Rus of Halich. But to the men of the Korzets party they were understandable, since upon the steppe one meets all men and one speaks all tongues. And the words were these:

### THE SONG OF THE TSIGANI

*Steppewide, starwide, on our track we roam*
*From the east to the western pale;*
*The rivers are our brothers and the woods our home*
*And the hills return our "Hail!"*
*Our cities are in ruins but we like them so*
*For walls and roofs are chains;*
*We tread the friendly earth or we ride the "roads that go"*
*And we ask no pay for our pains.*

*South wind blowing on the steppe or height,*
*As free as you are we;*
*North wind gnawing with his icy bite*
*But fills our hearts with glee.*
*Where the River Ganges through its meadow pours*
*Or the Nile drops to the sea*
*Or the winding Dnieper through the rapids roars*
*There roam the Tsigani.*

*Age-old Kiev with its hundred spires*
*Sarai with Tartar sheen,*
*Burn like gold in the ruby fires*
*In the crown of our Tsigan Queen.*

*The Gypsy Camp*

(Ornaments from Armenian Gospel, 14th Century.)

# THE TSIGAN RAFT

*Our cities are in ruins but we like them so*
*While we wander o'er the Czarny Szlak;*
*We tread the friendly earth or we ride the "roads that go"—*
*Come and follow in the Tsigan track!*

"There lies the raft." One of the men pointed and whispered to the leader, Jan Korzets.

Out on the river, tugging at restraining ropes, was a large raft made of rough logs. The Tsigani must have worked long days to build it, for it was substantial and strongly lashed with thongs. Jan Korzets indicated by a nod of the head that it would exactly serve his purpose, and the whole company wheeled suddenly out from the trees that concealed them and approached the Tsigan band.

At sight of them the singing in the camp gave way to an uproar. Men leaped for their spears; women gathered up their babies and dashed to the wagons; the old hag who had been minding the kettle tore up the supports from the ground and hurried with it after them, the meat which had been cooking there emitting volumes of steam; horses catching the excitement neighed, orders ran from man to man—it was indeed a hurly-burly. But Jan Korzets, lifting up his voice, shouted in Polish:

"Peace be with you. I come on a peaceful errand."

A middle-aged man of intelligent cast of brow approached the riders quickly, scanned them carefully, and turned to the rest with the cry: "It is the Lechs. Jan Korzets leads them."

"Jan Korzets. Jan Korzets," the cry was repeated, and in a trice the alarm had died down. The middle-aged Tsigan coming close to the leader took his right hand and kissed it. And then the activity which had been going on in the camp when the horsemen came went on again as if nothing had happened. The men put down their spears, the children and women came bursting out

[ 25 ]

of the wagons, the old hag set back the kettle poles in the ground, over the fire, and the more curious ones crowded about the knights.

"It is you then, Stasko," exclaimed Michael's father.

"Yes. It is I. With my people, upon the Dniester, enroute for Kamenets. Is there anything in which I can serve you?"

"Indeed there is. I would have your people pole us across the river on your raft at sunset."

Stasko gazed at him curiously. "You are going to Halich?"

"I am."

"Then the raft is at your service. I have received too many favors from your father and yourself not to return them when I may." He put his fingers in his mouth and whistled. "How many are there in your party?"

"A dozen. We will pay you well."

And at once Stasko gave directions to his people to have the raft in readiness for the crossing. One of Korzets' archers went back for the rest of the company and the others threw themselves from their horses to the ground, where they were soon asleep beneath the shade of the trees, for it was just past mid-day now and the sun had been warm in the meadows through which they had traveled.

Michael slept too, but awakening before the others, he went roaming about the Tsigan camp. It was the first time he had ever come into an encampment of these people, of whom it was said in Poland that they were always marching but they never knew where. In early childhood he had been afraid of these swarthy folk with their ragged, though ribbon-bedecked garments, and their mysterious ways and talk, yet he had always felt the fascination that was theirs. Under the law they had rights in all countries in the world: in Poland they might camp for seven days upon any estate they chose, but at the end of seven days they must depart under penalty of severe punishment. As the boy strolled about the camp the men smiled at him and the women threw kisses at him, for the word had gone about quickly that he was a Korzets and a friend of wanderers. Bright eyes gazing out at him from tangled mats of hair seemed to bring about him more keenly the feeling that he was walking in a dream, the feeling of unreality that had come upon him since the King's words of the night before.

Beyond the wagons were a few small tents, where no doubt, he thought, women and children were sleeping; the tents themselves were of rags and of practically no protection from weather or rain, but they did serve as a slight shelter, and perhaps gave privacy to the women and their children. From several of these were thrust out the thick foot coverings of the women—mere wrappings of hide and bark; from others bare feet protruded. But at some little distance beyond the other tents was one from which no feet protruded; there was nothing about it unusual in any way, and yet something drew him over to it. He could not tell why exactly—in fact, he never knew, but it was part of the same magic that surrounded him from the beginning until the end of all things in Halich. He made his way toward this last tent slowly, curiously, musing—and then suddenly a voice leaped out of the tent—its accents thrilled him—the words were pure Polish.

"Come here."

He went over to it and looked down. And then through the end of the tent was thrust a laughing, swarthy face. It was the face of a girl or a boy of his own age, perhaps a little younger— the hair was yellow, the eyes blue.

"Go over behind those trees," a nod of the head indicated the place; "I will join you in an instant. . . . Quick. . . . Do not let them see you talking to me."

In a daze, yet with quick action, he slipped behind the trees; there were three of them, close together, one with a large trunk;

it was impossible for the Tsigani to see him there. He waited but an instant.

A lithe body shot swiftly along the ground and dropped, with legs curled beneath it, at the base of one of the trees. "There," it exclaimed, "I am sure that no one saw me. . . . Can you see anyone looking this way?"

Michael peeped around a tree trunk. "No. They are busy with the raft," he replied. And then he looked down at his merry companion in astonishment. For though the creature was dressed as a boy, in a short leather jacket and coarse, ragged hose that fitted close to the legs, the face was certainly the face of a girl, and to prove it at that instant long locks of yellow hair that gleamed like gold fluttered down and fell about her eyes. She brushed the hair aside and looked up at him, the eyebrows above her blue eyes were nearly joined in a continuous line, her features were finely cut—she was unmistakably a Slav.

"Who are you?" blurted Michael in astonishment.

"My name is Katerina."

"You are not a Tsiganka (gypsy girl)?"

"No. . . . Indeed my mother was Polish."

He was silent momentarily, knowing not what to say.

"And you are of the family of Jan Korzets. I heard the Tsigani say that."

"My name is Michael. . . . But what are you doing here in this camp? Have the Tsigani carried you away?"

"No." She became grave immediately. "I will tell you, but you must promise not to tell. . . . I am a prisoner, but not against my will."

"A prisoner?" Michael picked up the word quickly. "Then let me bring my father and his men here. They will free you at once. Does Stasko know that you are here?"

"Yes. He brought me. And you must not tell your father,

for as I said, though I am a prisoner, yet I am not a prisoner against my will."

Her voice was soft and low and it sounded in Michael's ears like the wind in the trees.  There was something in her gentility and natural grace that was unfamiliar to him, for he had seen little of gentlefolk in the courts, and these qualities shone through the dingy, mud-stained garments that she wore and the dark stain that had been rubbed into her skin.  There was that about her which drew him imperatively to serve her; a childish charm, perhaps, that enkindled nobility in him.

"Tell me your story," he said.

"I know not where to begin. . . .  My mother died when I was a child and that was fourteen years ago.  She came of a Krakow family.  My father I have never seen.  I am on my way to join him now."

"But in these clothes?  And with these people?  Surely they are but a poor escort?"

"The gypsy disguise is necessary.  As for these people, they are not bad.  Indeed there is not a better guide in all Poland than this Stasko. . . .  I was brought up in Chelm after my mother died in a Tartar raid. . . .  My father was carried a prisoner to Suzdal where because of his nobility he was released by orders of the Khan himself.  The sisters in a convent in Chelm took care of me, and taught me what they themselves knew.  I have been very happy with them and have but recently left them."

"Why did you leave them?"

"My father sent word that I was to come to him in Halich."

"And you were not afraid to leave the convent and come with strange men through a strange country to see a father whose face you could not remember?"

"I have no fear.  Besides, he is my father."

"But to travel in this fashion?"

[ 29 ]

"Stasko is an old friend to us all. Often while I was in the convent he brought news to me of my father, and carried messages."

"But why this secrecy?"

"That I do not know. . . . Michael—you say your name is Michael?" He nodded and she resumed, "There is something strange about all of this, something that I do not understand. Some mystery that Stasko knows not of, or if he knows will not tell me. . . . What are you doing here?"

The question caught him unawares. "I am upon a mission."

"And is the mission a secret one?"

He bowed his head in assent.

"I knew it!" she exclaimed. "I knew it!"

"Knew what?" he asked.

"That you—Poles—in armor are here upon the same mysterious errand as I. . . . How do I know? . . . By this and by that. . . . For why should you come here upon a secret mission, and why should I come here upon a secret mission? . . . Michael," she exclaimed fervently—"I need a friend. I say that I am not afraid—but I fear lest something that is unknown, something terrible that is beyond my thoughts, might happen. You are going to Halich and so am I. If I see you there and need help, will you help me or bring help to me?"

"I will. I will," he promised.

Then all at once her mood became more playful. "There is adventure in this," she said, "and excitement comes upon me all the time. Yet I feel safe with Stasko, for he is wary and cunning, and though we have been stopped many times by bodies of armed men, he has always concealed me. Indeed the Tsigan disguise is enough. . . . But speak to me in Polish again. I have not heard that language for so long."

"What language will you speak in Halich?"

"The language of Rus."

"Then your father is of Rus?"

"Of the old family of Roman and Danilo, a descendant of Lev the founder of Lvov, and he himself bears the name of Lev."

Then upon Michael fell a shadow. He shuddered, and it seemed somehow as if the cloud that had come across the sun came also across the brightness of his own thoughts. But after that came the sense of magic again, the spell—it seemed impossible that he, Michael Korzets, should be here in this wood by the bank of the Dniester conversing with this girl who told of such wonderful things. For the name Lev, the Greek for Lion, had not been known in the Red Land for years; it was thought that it had died out when Kazimir took over the border provinces many years before. But he only asked:

"Then there is nothing we can do?"

"Not now. But I may call upon you when the time arrives. I must see my father. If he is what I think, then I shall remain with him. If he is not, then I shall ask your father and you to take me away."

Impulsively he demanded: "And may we not do that now? You go to a man whom you do not know. Indeed there is trouble in Halich," he looked directly into her face, "and no man knows what will be the end of it. I know, and yet I do not know how I know, that there is nothing there but trouble for you. And indeed what can there be? The old city is in ruins, the new city is only being built, and with but slight protection there is danger from the Lithuanians or Tartars. Will you not come with me now to my father, and he will see that you have safe escort back to Lvov."

She shook her head. "It is pleasant," she said, "to hear you wish me so well. But what I must do I will do. And I must go to Halich."

"Then how may we know if you need our help?"

"Stasko will bring word. He is attached to me, I think, and will do what I ask."

There came a loud cry from the river; the raft was out on the current and the men were leaping aboard it after assembling their horses and returning for arms and supplies. All the Tsigani rowers were ranged about the edge of the raft, their muscles tense as they shoved with long poles to propel the craft from the bank.

"I must go," exclaimed Michael, "though I know that I shall see you again."

"Until then," she said. He kissed her hand as he had been taught to kiss the hand of elders and though she was not an elder, yet he felt impelled to accord her the same honor; then leaping away and running, he hurled himself upon the raft just in time, for in a moment more the distance between it and the shore would have been too great.

The sun in the west was now turning red as the raft swung out into the current and was poled slantingly across toward the south bank. Over the distant hills a blue haze was beginning to rise; birds were singing and now the Tsigani joined them:

> *Our cities are in ruins but we like them so,*
> *For walls and roofs are chains;*
> *We tread the friendly earth or we ride the "roads that go"*
> *And we ask no pay for our pains.*

# CHAPTER III

## IN THE HANDS OF AN ENEMY

AS the raft idled out into the current Michael caught one fleeting glance of a flash of gold in the Tsigan camp that betokened that Katerina had gone back to her tent; the other Tsigani were busily packing up their possessions in preparation to moving down the bank a little way, for it was impossible that the raft should be poled back to its original place and they wished to locate their encampment close to it. The raft would slant across the river and land the Poles, and then it would slant back to their side again but at a point farther down, possibly at the very edge of the wood. As he looked downstream and ahead, the whole lay-out of the ancient city came to him much more clearly than it had before, set as it was between two rivers to west and east, and facing the third river on the north. Over their heads almost, towered the hill which bore the church of Pantalemon, though the raft swung in under it quickly and the tower could not be seen.

They landed just to the west of the river Tchev, at the point where it joins the Dniester, for here, as Stasko knew, there was firm footing for the horses on a short, pebbly beach; by dint of pulling and much cajoling these were led off the landward side of the raft, and driven up the slope to pasture-land where they at once fell to feeding. It was rapid business, the landing, and in a very short time the raft was off again for the opposite shore, with

Stasko kissing his hand to Jan Korzets. The men mounted the
horses and rode across the pasture-land by the foot of a high hill,
and then turned to the left into a wooded glade. Here a halt was
called.

The place was well chosen. Fresh water trickled down in a
tiny stream at their feet to join the river not far distant; a few
fallen trees directly in front made a formidable barricade in case
of attack. And it was evident that Jan Korzets had the pos-
sibility of an attack in his head, for he set the men to piling other
logs upon the fallen trees and to heaping up the crevices between
with brush and twigs. Those who were not thus aiding in
strengthening the fortifications loosened their heavy garments
and spent a space in dozing while the archers were absent in
search of game. Later when they returned, well-laden, a fire
was already roaring in the midst of the camp and soon the odor of
cooking meat came with much welcome to the nostrils of the
hungry men.

As they sat eating, Michael's father talked of the events of
the day. "I wonder if that Tsigan, Stasko, is right," he said.
"He told me that this country is full of armed men, with more
coming daily. And yet we have not seen even a trace of one.
I don't know what to make of it. I had hoped to run across someone ere now who could tell me something, but as it is, all is wrapped
in mystery."

Stefan of Tarnov, who had ridden beside Jan Korzets for many
years, asked, "Had Stasko seen these men?"

"Yes. He had. He saw pointed helmets, and that means
Tartars. The men with robes of animals were Lithuanians.
The men with the long-poled axes were from Moskva or Suzdal.
. . . And then he has seen others, men in heavy mail, long black
corselets, helmets with pointed visors—I know of no such people in
this land. Normans they might be, or Hungarians perhaps,

though the Hungarians wore no such armor when I was last in Peth."

"Had he seen any ships on the river?"

"Yes—and that is curious. You know the old ships we used to find on these rivers, the old Slavic galleys? Well, these are nothing of that kind. These are of polished wood, well-armored, richly decorated; the sails are heavy, of costly cloth. In shape, too, they are not like our ships."

"But where are they? We saw no galleys as we crossed on the raft."

"They are below the bridge at the foot of the town, and around the bend of the river. . . . Stasko has an opinion in this matter which I do not share. Still, he has traveled much. He may be right, though it seems incredible. . . . From the point where the galleys are moored, it is about an hour's journey across the meadows to Krylos Hill."

Michael listened eagerly to the conversation that followed; of fear he had none since he had been brought up from childhood in the midst of raids and alarms of war. And particularly in this group of frontier knights he felt the greatest security, since they were all seasoned by wars on the steppe. Next to actual adventure, which was to them the spice of life, they liked best the exchange of stories, about the camp fires of an expedition. In this they indulged now until a late hour while the men posted for duty kept watch at the outer limits of the camp.

"I remember this place twenty years ago," said a grizzled old warrior, after many tales had been told. "There were some few descendants of the families of the boyars of old Rus here then, and they were constantly fighting with the Lithuanians. That is, they were fighting with them except at such times as Tartars appeared and then they both forgot their own quarrels and turned on the Tartar."

"That was before our King came here?"

"Yes. The boyars were a valiant lot, full of fight, and if Lithuanian or Tartar were not about they were forever fighting among themselves. They loved conspiracies above all things; daggers, poisons, treachery of all kinds, and they were, I think, the most jealous people on earth. Why, if there were two brothers in a family, and a stranger should praise one brother to the other, the one who was not praised would go into a furious rage, and like as not a war would be the result. In the beginning, when he had driven out the pagans, our King tried to make this an independent province, but the ruling family of Romanovs poisoned each other off in such numbers that he had to step in and appoint his own governor. That was the house of the descendants of Roman of Volynia, of Danilo his son, and of Lev his son. True boyars all of them and great men."

"Have the Poles always been in here?"

"Yes and no. In the beginning Vladimir of Kiev drove out the Lechs, or ancestors of the Poles, from this district, but they came back with Boleslas and retook their homes. During the wars with the boyars they came and went alternately, and during the reign of the Hungarians they came back in great numbers. It was a princess of Poland, Salomea, who was married to the Hungarian king Koloman in that cathedral on Krylos, but the boyars soon drove them out."

"Do you think that the wars will cease now that the country has come to Poland?"

Michael's father answered. "That I hope. But who can tell? We are here upon the frontier of that which men call civilization."

They took deep draughts of the cool air and began to yawn in the midst of their words. The smoke-scent of the wood fire stung their eyes with a desire for sleep. And giving way, they spread over themselves the blankets which the horses did not require and were soon snoring.

Michael lay with open eyes beneath the corner of his blanket, listening to the snapping of the fire, and watching the stars through the tree branches, his mind throbbing with the pictures of the deeds of valor recounted by these men, and his own imagination coloring for him other pictures in which he himself was the hero. At length the fire died down and there were only glowing coals.

About midnight the guard at the spring saw by the light of the stars a body of men on horseback riding swiftly and noiselessly across the meadows by the river edge. He shouted an alarm. Michael's father came running while the others sprang to their feet and tightened their coats.

"See: off to the west, perhaps half a mile."

"Tartars. No others ride like that. There must be an hundred of them. . . . Quick," he shouted to the others, "mount your horses and ride back over the ground we have covered. We will follow the Tchev valley and circle about the city to the bridge."

They rode silently over the soft turf to the edge of the wood, then turned to the right along an old trail that followed the Tchev to the south. For the moment Jan Korzets believed that the Tartars had been left safely behind them, but the belief was sadly shattered the next moment, when, with loud shouts and clashing of armor, a scouting party of Tartars in advance of the main body dashed up from the meadow bordering the river and fell upon the Poles from the rear.

"Destroy. Kill," went up the shouts.

Michael threw himself flat upon his horse's back to escape a sudden flight of arrows. He had been the last to leave the camp and was riding at a short distance behind the last member of his own party. The missiles came with such suddenness that the horse took fright momentarily at the whirring of shafts over his head, even though he was trained to border warfare. But Michael dug in with his spurs and the animal sank back upon his haunches and then in an excess of violent motion leaped ahead with terrific energy. He did not collide with the horse ahead, however, for that in turn was racing along the turf-covered road as if a thousand burrs were under its saddle.

"Single file," shouted Jan Korzets and the command was passed along until it reached Michael.

Through the night they raced, knowing that their only safety lay in speed; to turn and engage the scouting party behind meant certain death, for while they were skirmishing, the main detachment would come up and they would be surrounded. But just as they reached a point where they believed that for the moment they had gained a little on their pursuers, there came shouting of a nature similar to that which they had heard behind, only this time the shouting came from the road ahead.

"No other way," shouted the leader. "Fight your way through."

And they charged directly into the midst of another Tartar scouting party of perhaps a dozen men.

Clash—clash—steel against steel and the crashing of bodies to the ground. Hacking, pounding, smashing their way through, the Poles drove back the Tartar ranks, spilling the lighter riders from their saddles and driving the heavier-armed men into a compact mass on either side. The Poles had the distinct advantage in that their horses had been dashing along the road so rapidly, while the Tartars, though descending a hill, had really reined in their horses to wait for the Polish soldiers, whom they thought they had easily at their mercy by reason of the pressure of the other band from the rear. But in a furious moment the Poles had cut their way through as if they were madmen, and were off again up the sloping road that followed the river, while the pursuers, coming up from behind at the same instant, collided with the second band of their own men and were forced to slow down in order to restore order out of confusion.

"Everyone is safe," exclaimed the man ahead of Michael, as he took hasty count of the riders. "Only Tartars fell in that collision."

"So—so," replied Michael, exulting, rising up in his stirrups to peer ahead; but at that very second his horse stepped into a hole, floundered—crash—he had fallen directly across the path; and this while the man in front, having but just accounted for all the members of his party satisfactorily, had spurred his horse ahead at full speed. Michael had tried to shout, but an overhanging limb had made him duck his head suddenly, and the shout was lost. He had grasped at the limb in desperation, but missed it, and the next second had been thrown clear off his horse. He had felt himself falling; his head struck something so that he seemed to hear it crack, and then darkness fell upon his senses and he lay by the road in the direct path of the oncoming Tartars, and not one member of his own party realized that he was not with them in safety.

When he came to, a bright light was shining in his eyes. His head was shrieking with pain and he tried to raise his hands to it but found that he could not move them. They were lashed to his side by a Tartar lariat. He tried to kick, but another lariat was about his legs. Then, as the circumstances of his fall rushed into his head, he shuddered and a prayer rose to his lips; for as his eyes grew accustomed to the light and he glanced about, he saw that he was lying, bound hand and foot, in front of a huge fire, and that he was surrounded by Tartars!

Directly opposite was squatted their leader, perhaps a lesser khan. He was short like the rest, dark, with hair in braids, clad not in skins of animals as men described Tartars, but in a long garment of scarlet cloth upon which were plated shining plaques of armor, and his legs were encased in leggings covered with metal. His eyes were dark, the moustache long and braided, and upon his head was the pointed helmet that made the Tartar known from afar. Near him were other men similarly attired though in lesser degree of sumptuousness and they were conversing about him or taking orders, for every now and then they nodded toward him or illustrated a phrase by gesticulation in his direction.

Then a sudden interrogation struck Michael's brain like a blow. What had become of his father and the rest of the party? Had they escaped?

He pondered for a moment, cast his eyes about to see if any other forms were lying bound like himself near the fire. None. They had escaped. And then there came to him the thought which burst like a fountain in his brain—hope—they would rescue him!

After that he felt less apprehension. And yet the Tartars were not pleasant to look upon. Nature had chiseled out their faces with a look of imperturbability that was of the East, and the dark skins that seemed baked upon their bodies suggested cruelty. . . . But they would come to rescue him. . . . They would come to rescue him. . . . Yet, just how long had he been unconscious, and where was he now? He looked about him—there were no trees near at hand. They must be near the river bank, but he dared not turn fully around lest he attract too much attention.

All at once orders rang out. The darkness was lifting a little and the breezes of approaching dawn were on his face, and the birds were beginning to sing. Soldiers rushed up and extinguished the fire. There was the sound of hoofs thundering upon the ground. A body of men swept by. He could see, even in the mist of the early dawn, how easily they rode, swaying gracefully in their saddles as if they were part of their horses. Only a few wore skins, most of them wore heavy robes plated with metal; some were even in armor woven of light chain, and all carried swords, bows, and spears.    To the horses' bridles were attached small shields, shields with pointed centers that all at once picked up the rays of the rising sun and tossed the light about.

Someone stood him on his feet.    He felt cramped, sore, and dizzy.    But he knew that he must convey the idea of absolute obedience to his captors unless he wished to draw hostile attention. The bonds of his legs and arms were loosened, but another lariat was slipped over his head and about his waist, drawn up fairly tight but not tight enough to cause pain.    He was to be led along, he reasoned, knowing the method by which the Tartars brought in captives, and a prayer rose to his lips that the journey would not be long nor the pace too swift, for that was one way to death.

There came a twitch at the rope about his waist and he walked ahead.    The Tartar who held the other end of the lariat was in no way different from the other members of the party; he rode a small horse, sharp of nose, and long of mane and tail, nervous and rather spirited.    But the rider kept a close rein upon it, and Michael could easily keep up with the slow-moving column by proceeding at a simple walk.

Suddenly the mist rolled away ahead of them and they were at the bank of a small stream, the Tchev.    Through this the horses waded.    Michael followed, prepared at any moment to swim, but the river bed remained firm beneath his feet; it seemed like the place of an old ford.    He scrambled up the farther bank where a much-used and ancient road led up a slope between two hills; at the top of the slope were the ruins of an old gate and walls, a rounded arch and wooden rampart, and then suddenly the whole plain lay open before them.

For a moment Michael forgot his predicament and peril in the realization of what lay ahead.    He was looking down directly upon the remains of the old city of Halich. Of this there could be no doubt.

This was the ancient capital of the Slav world. Here in old days the boyars and the heroes fought with the Hungarians and the men of Novgorod and Kiev; this road which lay ahead down the hill was once a street that echoed the hoof beats of thousands of horses and camels, and perhaps even the tramping of elephants. Now—the broken walls squatted like ugly things in the glory of the morning sun; beams rotted with decay perched here and there over leaning poles or crumbling bricks. Great yawning holes betokened the former presence of houses and dwors (noblemen's homes); as they descended the hill wild animals slunk away from them and ran off into the ruins, and now and then a furtive dweller in the wreckage peered at the Tartars in terror from behind a mass of heaped-up stone, or fled with precipitation through crumbling blocks of brick and mortar to disappear in some subterranean hole. But the Tartars did not trouble them. They were not in Halich on an expedition of plunder.

Far off to the left rose the majestic roof of the Tserkiev, St. Pantalemon, which he had seen from the river; it rose amidst a cluster of tree tops, beautiful and majestic, with a Greek dome that proclaimed its Byzantine ancestry. It alone of the more important buildings in the lower grod had been spared. Long windows reaching down from the dome, once graced with marvelous glass, were now empty.

Off ahead, with the sun glinting over the ruins of Halich, appeared the division of streets and avenues as they had been of old. Many of the wooden buildings had utterly disappeared, and in their places rose peasant cottages with thatched roofs, cottages of the Karaite people perhaps, a tribe that, professing Judaism, also accepted Christ as the divine prophet of the great Jehovah. They had brought with them in their migration many curious customs;

they wore clothes all of wool, or all of cotton—they never mixed textures.

On and on they went, descending constantly by the road which crossed the expanse of this vast old capital.  Soon far ahead on the distant hills which rose above the River Lukiev at the eastern extremity of the town could be seen the ruins of an old watch tower, upon which men were working; at that distance they looked like ants, and the boards they were raising looked like small sticks.

But as they approached this watch tower, the Tartars swung to the right and followed a road that ran south along the bank of the Lukiev.  As they went along, Michael noticed that the peasants' cottages here were all closed and the doors barred, as if the inhabitants were in hiding; nor did he see any peasants at work in the fields, nor were any wagons upon the road.  The only signs of life, besides the marching Tartars, were the wild animals in the bushes and the little lizards that ran along the edge of the road.

The sun rose higher and higher, and now they were moving through what was once a very densely populated section.  Here and there were the ruins of old churches and tserkievs, palaces and fortresses, for in old days Halich had as many towers as did "Mother" Kiev or "Lord" Novgorod.  They had marched in a southerly direction for about three miles when suddenly the Tartars shouted in concert; Michael had no way of knowing what they said, but as he looked ahead, straining at his leash to get a better view, he saw the reason.

There it was, Krylos: the hill which bore upon its summit the proud towers of the Church of Our Mother of God, and not only was there a church, a cathedral, but a combined palace and castle as well, surrounded by huge walls and guarded by towers in front. All about rose the ruins of the mansions of old days, the days when Roman or Danilo held court on the height, or the day when King Koloman married Salomea the Polish princess.  It was a very city in itself, and indeed the hill Krylos was the old ducal city, Halich—for when in very old times men spoke of Halich they meant the land where behind walls stood the Cathedral and the palaces. The lower city was but an appendage to it: Krylos, with its richly mosaic Cathedral, was the jewel, the place of treasures, and though pillaged and looted, still held its walls and towers upright after all these years.

The Tartars went along below the hill for about a mile, then turning to the left crossed the Lukiev at a ford and mounted the slope toward the old city. The ascent was steep and the horses went slowly, but Michael on his leash toiled painfully.

"I wonder what can be in wait for me?" he thought over and over again. Now that the destination seemed near, he felt weary unto death almost, hungry, thirsty and full of pain. The lariat had begun to compress his chest, and his legs ached for they had traveled some six or seven miles; but he fought off discouragement, for he was proud, and he was shrewd too in that he knew that if he gave way to weakness no pity would be shown him.

Suddenly a huge gate loomed before him, or rather the ruins of a gate that had once been a thing of magnificence. In old days men had called it the German gate either in honor of the German emperor Barbarossa or because great bodies of German settlers and traders had come to Halich. Some semblance of a gate hung now between two wooden towers; the portcullis had long since rusted—at a challenge the gate swung back and the horsemen passed through. They ascended to the top of the hill by a road grown over with grass, turned to the left where rose the tower of the Cathedral, and passed a partly ruined building which had once been the residence of the princes, or perhaps the boyars of their druzina or family circle.

In spite of his fatigue, Michael eagerly drank in all there was to see, since the story of the magnificent city of Halich and its utter destruction had always captivated his boyish imagination.

Yet here, instead of the stagnation he had always visualized, there was a very fever of construction in progress. Workmen were putting stones in place, dragging in new-hewed beams, extending timbers across roofless walls, or bolstering up the walls themselves. Many of the buildings, which must have stood in magnificent ruins for years, were being made habitable; the cathedral, now fully restored, seemed almost as it might have been in the old days.

And then there swarmed out of one of the buildings to meet the Tartars another race of men. The leader who came forward was a giant in stature, over six feet high, with dark hair and eyes, the eyebrows nearly joined. The skin was darkly pigmented—the eyes, almond-shaped, were like wells of fire; his arms and legs were long; a rich coat fell from shoulder to knees; the boots were red and high; he wore no head covering for the moment so that his dark hair fell in ringlets about his face and neck. There was something in his countenance that was fine, imperial even—there was courage and culture written upon his features, and understanding lived in the lines of his forehead.

Coming forward quickly he saw Michael on the leash; a scowl played over his features. "Cut the cords," he commanded, accompanying the words which he spoke in the language of Rus with a violent gesture.

The Tartars did not understand the words but they did understand the motion of his arm. And as they unloosed the thongs and freed him from the lariat, Michael's heart leaped up in a prayer of thanksgiving, for he knew that in the fine eyes of the man who seemed to be the commander of them all was an assurance that there was nothing to fear; indeed, the man had such nobility and carriage that one might put implicit trust in him at the very first sight. This the boy did. But as the rope fell away, there came over him a great exhaustion, and hunger and thirst. Something in his heart snapped, and darkness fell over him. He was conscious of falling to the ground.

# CHAPTER IV

## THE DEN OF THE LION

WHEN he awoke from the heavy sleep that had followed his loss of consciousness in the courtyard, darkness had fallen upon the earth in good earnest. It was not wholly dark, however; a yellow and red burning torch was throwing its light by leaps and starts about the room, a torch located somewhere outside, probably in a corridor; it was a high room, he could see that, and as he looked directly upward, for he was lying on his back upon a hard bed, the shadows danced aside for a moment and he could see that the ceiling was sagging and the walls bulging, though patched here and there with new boards. But all at once a feeling of terrific thirst and hunger struck him like a blow; he cried out, overcome with the pain of it, and to his amazement someone came up to him out of the darkness and in a not unkind voice asked in the language of Rus if he desired food and drink.

"I do," he cried, and the figure hurried away.

He returned with fresh meat and bread, and water in a copper bowl. Michael fell upon these ravenously. It was not until he finished that he looked about again, and then with senses a little less confused, since his hunger was now satisfied.

"Where am I? Where am I? Where am I?" he thought.

It was necessary then to piece out the whole story, which at length passed through his brain like pictures in a dream.

# THE DEN OF THE LION

Finally, "Then I must be a prisoner in the castle on Krylos Hill. How can I let my father know that I am alive?"

He arose from the bed which occupied the left-hand corner of the room, farthest from the entrance. There was no door to the room now, but bars had been thrown across the opening, holding the occupant a prisoner. Michael walked about over the careening floor, where men had evidently been working recently, shivering a little, for the night air was chill. On one side of the room two long, narrow windows looked out to the stars. He put his head through one and saw by the starlight the River Lukiev just below him, and in the distance the hills over the Tchev. Upward the wall stretched away a long distance; he was evidently on a lower floor of the castle. But no man, nor boy even, could squeeze through those windows which had been cut out of solid stone centuries before—they were wide enough for his head but the shoulders must certainly stick, and then too it was a sheer drop to the river. No one could make that and remain unhurt.

"What will they think? What will they think?" he asked himself as he turned away from the window. "My father must believe that I am dead. . . . They probably never missed me until they had gone some miles. . . . I was the last in the company. . . . They must have gone back to look for me. . . . And not finding me. . . ." Then he thought of his fallen horse—"I wonder if the horse was killed? If they went back and found the horse after the Tartars had taken me away, they would certainly think that I was dead, or a prisoner. . . . What would they do then?" He tried to weigh both sides of the question as his father would have weighed it—the King's errand on one side, the safety of the son on the other. "They must be near here," he reasoned. Then he wondered again why they had not returned to the Tartars' camping place, where he had been taken after his capture, ready to strike and make a rescue if possible, for these men of the steppe did not fear death, and his father would gladly have given his life for his son. "He must know that I am safe," was the answer that blazed in his brain. "Otherwise he would have made an attack upon the Tartars either at their camping place or later when they were traveling to Halich."

His questioning was cut short at this point by the entrance of the man who had brought him the food and water. He carried a torch in one hand so that Michael could see plainly what sort of man he was. He was a servant, there was no mistaking that; he wore a leather jacket with broad collar folded down, the lower fringe of the jacket falling halfway between thigh and knee. His legs were bare, and rough sandals were tied about the ankles in the manner in which men tie the necks of bags of meal.

He spoke to Michael.

"Have you eaten?"

"I have."

"Then be pleased to come with me." He bowed and pointed to the door.

Michael asked, "Whither?"

"To the Duke. He gave orders that you were to be brought before him as soon as you were awake and had eaten."

He went ahead through the door. Michael found himself in a corridor smelling of new-cut boards. Old charred planking lay about in piles where it had been hauled down. New doors were being fitted to chambers, certain decorations that had lost their color were being retouched—all about, the whole palace was being restored after it had stood empty for many years. As they marched along he saw that room after room was already furnished with rebuilt ceiling and floor—it must have taken a small forest to supply the lumber that lay about; truly the work of renovation was going on apace.

Finally the servant opened a small door at the end of the corridor and pushed the boy inside a room. He followed behind him and drew the door to without a noise.

"Wait your turn. You will be called," the servant whispered in his ear, drawing him close to the wall where for the moment they would remain unobserved.

Michael stared as if in a dream upon the scene in front of him.

The door had admitted them to a large room, dome-shaped, lighted by the fires that leaped from four huge braziers burning about an immense throne. This throne was mounted on a platform in the middle of the room, directly beneath the center of the dome. Upon the throne, which seemed to be of light wood, or perhaps ivory, sat a kingly figure, clad in a rich magnificence that was Oriental in luxury, and graced with both dignity and splendor. A long cape of blue was thrown over an inner coat of richly embroidered cloth, which, caught in at the waist by a tight silken belt, fell to the ankles in horizontal pleats. Gold and silver ornaments rich with embossing shone upon his dress when rays of light fell upon them; his sandals of soft leather were bound with several turns of deerhide thongs. About him stood a semicircle of armed men, with light chain armor that showed fringes of metal at knee and throat, beneath rich outer garments.

But it was not the Duke that most impressed Michael; it was not the crowd nor the soldiers nor the rich mosaics of the dome and walls—mosaics which delineated heraldic designs, a knight in mail, a jackdaw on a field of white, and a lion leaping at the stars; that which impressed the boy was the tall figure that stood in front of the Duke—a man of gigantic stature, clad all in white, with a tall, pointed hat upon his head. A feeling of strange familiarity invested itself somehow in this man, his height, his moustache and beard bristling in the shape of a cross.

"Where have I seen him before?" Michael wondered.

There was magic in the room. The braziers burned fitfully,

[ 49 ]

THE GOLDEN STAR OF HALICH

tossing their light unevenly and in many-colored flames; overhead the Byzantine dome and its mosaic figures looked down curiously, the features of the men represented there, twisting and taking grotesque shapes in the varying light. A deep silence hung over the company until the tall man spoke.

"Your birth and your life are governed by the sign of the Lion in the Heavens," he began, "for your name is Lev and Lev is Leo. You were born when the sun was in the house of the Lion and those so born are great of heart."

He held up his right hand, and in it was a rod that threw off gleaming reflections from the fires of the braziers. And Michael, leaning forward, noticed that in the space in front of the ducal throne there stood curious instruments, a huge globe of red and yellow stone, two large inverted copper bowls, a brass sphere surrounded by circular rings and metal fastened to the sphere by projections. On a computing board bright against the light of one of the lamps was a square containing numbers. The numbers were these:

| 13 | 3  | 2  | 16 |
|----|----|----|----|
| 12 | 6  | 7  | 9  |
| 8  | 10 | 11 | 5  |
| 1  | 15 | 14 | 4  |

arranged in the form of a square.

"Continue, Phokas," said the Duke.

# THE DEN OF THE LION

And at the name, all the surmises and suspicions that had lain within Michael's brain suddenly ran together. Phokas—he an astrologer, for such his garb and words proclaimed him; Lev, the Duke. That Phokas was the man who stood beside the dwarf in the market place in Lvov when he had thrown the dagger at Kazimir. That Duke Lev upon the throne was the man who had taken him from the Tartars earlier in the day. This castle was his, being rebuilt for occupancy, and all about were soldiers, Tartars, men of Rus, boyars, and many others that one knew not of. This was the plot that the King came to Lvov to discuss, and almost paid for that visit with his life.

But—Phokas is speaking again.

"It was for this that my master sent me here from Tsargrad," he went on. "He himself is a reader of the stars, and he and I have studied together for many years. And though he knew that misfortune was to come upon himself, during these days while he is in Thrace, yet he knows by the stars that he is to be redeemed, and is to become master of the Eastern Roman Empire again."

"And believing in that he sent you here?"

"He did. And more with me. For there have come galleys from that proud city which as Byzantium or the city of Constantine once ruled the whole civilized world. And in the galleys which came hither with me were soldiers from all the Eastern Empire, Greeks, Macedonians and Slavs. And on the day when the stars are in conjunction, your star and his, then he will come himself."

"Is that time far off?"

"It lacks but two days."

"How did your master know of me?"

"He knows all things. He knew that you were a descendant of Roman and Danilo, and that the time was ripe for you to sit upon the ducal throne of your ancestors; therefore he summoned you from Suzdal."

# THE GOLDEN STAR OF HALICH

"And he trusts the stars?"

"He does. And there is one star that will redeem us all."

"And that is—?"

"The Golden Star, which men know as the Golden Star of Halich. And as the Golden Star will rule the Heavens, so will the counterpart of the Golden Star on earth rule all these kingdoms of ours. The Eastern Roman Empire may be great, but its emperor will be the subject of the Golden Star; the Tartar Horde may rule the steppes, but the supreme one above them will be the Star; the ducal grod of Halich will be mighty, but it will be subject to the Star; the land of Rus and Lithuania will also be subject to the Star as the stars in the Heavens will be subject."

Michael's brain whirled. About him in the room the excitement was growing more and more intense; these who made up the crowd were the leaders of the plot, the generals, captains—men of Rus, descendants of the old boyars, and these others from foreign lands.

"In all these days of trouble," went on Phokas, "men in the Eastern world have watched the Heavens for the Golden Star. And it is the knowledge of those who read the Heavens that the Golden Star will come when the sun is in the House of the Lion. In old days the sun rose in different Houses at the twelve seasons of the year—different Houses from those which he now occupies in the twelve seasons. Yet when the Chaldeans computed the Houses, the House of the Lion was nearer midsummer or July. Now it is later, and the change comes with the middle of the month rather than at the beginning."

"But can man be certain that the stars determine his destiny?"

"He can. Life runs in cycles of eighteen years. Eighteen years ago a comet appeared in the sky and disappeared in your House, the constellation Leo, which is the House of the Sun. It was in that year that my master knew that one who bore the name Leo would in eighteen years be the powerful force in our plans."

The Duke broke out passionately: "How can I believe that all this is true? How can I believe that what goes on in the sky affects the lives of men? Have I not a soul answerable to God for what I do in the independence of my heart? Am I a slave to all those dots of light?"

Phokas smiled; this time it was a cruel smile, cold, almost savage, but Lev was not looking at him. Only Michael saw, and shuddered. "This is the wisdom of the wisest. It has been so from the beginning that men's lives are reflected from the stars above, whether we wish it or not. Otherwise men would all be alike on earth."

He waited as if inviting the Duke to speak again, but Lev had ceased watching him; he sat with his right arm braced on the arm of the throne, his head upon his hand.

"As it is, men differ from each other," went on the astrologer. "They are the same in those qualities which are reflected from the fixed stars; they differ in the things governed by those stars which are constantly changing their position. But that which is most important is this: there is a belt about the sky and in this belt which men call the Zodiac there are twelve Houses, each House represented by the figures which the stars within it form; there is the ram, the bull, the twins, the crab, the lion, the virgin, the scales, the scorpion, the archer, the goat, the waterbearer and the fishes. Each month the sun rises in one of these Houses, and in each House is a star which rules the destiny of that one who is born while the sun is in a particular House. Your House is a fortunate one, for the sun loves the House of the Lion, and you bear not only the good fortune of that House, but even the name Lion, or Lev, is yours."

He ceased. The Duke remained in meditation for a moment

until one of his druzina or knightly council stepped forward and whispered to him.

"Then the boy is here," he exclaimed. "Bring him forward."

Michael was trembling with excitement when they led him forward, through the astrologer's instruments and the guards, to an open space before the ducal throne. There were however two definite ideas in his head: one to petition his captor to send word to his father that he was alive; the other to escape as soon as possible from this place and carry the news of this coalition and conspiracy to the King.

"What is your name?" The Duke drew his eyebrows down hard.

"Michael. Of the Korzets crest."

"A good family. What do you, here in Halich?"

"I am a prisoner. The Tartars brought me."

"Then answer me freely. I would not harm you, and at the proper time you may depart."

"But," exclaimed Michael, stepping forward a pace or two, "will you not send word to my father that I am alive? He knows only that the Tartars took me captive. Had he known that I should be brought to you, he would have been greatly relieved, but as it is he must think that I am dead." He spoke with emotion; the place was silent save for the sputtering of fires on the braziers.

The Duke glanced about the company and his eyes fell upon a certain man. "Dimitri," he commanded, "tell me what you know of this boy's actions."

Dimitri, leather-clad, a warrior rather than a noble, came forward bowing profoundly. "This boy," he said, pointing, and speaking in a low tone as one who begins a long narrative, "was one of a company of Lechs or Poles who set out from Lvov two days ago for the city of Halich. I myself watched them on the road, and saw them ferried across the Dniester on a Tsigan raft.

Thinking that the excursion would bear watching I remained near them and saw them attacked by a scouting party from Sarai. This boy might have escaped with the others had his horse not fallen. Later when he was taken prisoner, I informed the chief of the detachment that he was not to be put to torture, but should be brought before you."

"What became of the others?"

"They followed the Tchev valley for many miles, not realizing that the boy was not with them, and it was only when they circled about to cross the plain from west to east that the leader, whose name is Jan Korzets, saw that the boy was not there. He then ordered the company to halt at once, and he himself with two others stole back to rescue the boy, if they could, by stealth; but it was daylight then and the Tartars had changed their position, and they finally returned to their party. I remained in hiding, watching them, ready to ride to you with information if anything should lead me to suspect that they were about to interfere with our plans."

"Did they learn what had become of the boy?"

"I think they did; for it was late in the afternoon when they made their way to the lower town and crossed back by the bridge. One of their scouts must have brought news that the boy was a prisoner here and had not been put to death, otherwise I feel certain that they would have remained. I followed them by the east road, and reported their movements to my chief; when we rode out after them they were heading for Bolshov as fast as their horses could carry them."

"Thank God then," burst forth Michael. "My father knows that I am safe here," and with that thought a great burden was lifted from his heart, and a curious sense of freedom and adventure came upon him.

But the Duke, leaning forward and dismissing the man who had brought the information, demanded sharply of the prisoner why he had come to Halich.

Michael was silent. Men on an errand for the King never betrayed their trust.

"Why have you come to Halich?" repeated the Duke.

"I may not answer," he said slowly. "The reason is not mine but another's."

The man scowled. He ran his fingers through his dark beard and cried out: "They have not crossed me yet, and they shall not cross me now. I hold to no quarrel with these Poles, and yet I hold to no peace with them."

"Then you should hold to a quarrel with them! It is they who stand in your way." These words came sharply from Phokas; he had been adjusting his instruments, apparently paying no attention to the conversation, though in truth he was taking in every word. "The Poles are your great enemies. The Turks are naught beside them." He came up by the side of Michael, threw at him a glance so withering that the boy shrank back, then leaping forward stood on the steps leading up to the throne and addressed both the Duke and the crowd:

"When I cast the horoscope of this leader of the house of Lev, there was one star in the north which baffled my course. Night after night and year by year I worked upon it; that star is Polaris and it is a star that is hostile. Its unfriendly rays will work ruin upon us unless we take heed of this warning which comes from Heaven itself."

His eyes blazed fire upon Michael; it was certain that he was the tall man in Lvov that day, and Michael knew that he now knew that Michael was the one who had frustrated the plot in Lvov. That he stood in great peril, the boy was quite aware, for it was apparently the astrologer's plan to incite the Duke to enmity against the Poles. He began to wonder how much the Duke knew of the attempt upon the life of Kazimir; as the man appeared to him brave, noble even, and serious, such a plot seemed not to be associated with him.  And then he realized, as Phokas spoke, that not only did the Duke not know of the plot in Lvov, but Phokas was striving to keep the knowledge from him.  Yes, the boy realized with triumph that in these words of Phokas there was a rancor so great as to cloak a fear, and the fear was that Michael should tell the Duke that he had been in Lvov and had seen the tall man with a dwarf who attempted to kill the King of Poland.  And more, that he had even heard the dwarf call the other "Phokas."

"Then what would you do?"  The Duke addressed the astrologer.

"Let me have the boy and I will force from him the nature of his mission here.  The times are threatening enough to us without unseen perils about.  If there is a company of Poles here, then they can be here for no good purpose."

The Duke made no answer.  Phokas continued: "Give the boy over to me, if even for a few hours.  I will find out what he has in his head."

Michael saw that the time for action had come unless he wished to be left to the mercy of Phokas.  "Your greatness," he exclaimed, his eyes flashing, his fists clenched, "give me not into the power of this man.  He would kill me even as he has wished to kill the King of Poland."

"What do you mean?"  The Duke rose to his feet.

"I mean," said Michael, "that this man and a dwarf were in Lvov not three days ago.  That the dwarf threw a knife at King Kazimir who had come to Lvov on a visit."

A very thundercloud of perplexity settled on the Duke's brows. Phokas threw back his head and roared in laughter.  "If you will deal with boys," he cried, "then you will have boys' imaginings.

. . . What dwarf went with me to Lvov? Do you know of any here? And as for throwing knives—did you say knives, boy? Three days ago? Did you not all know that I came here on a galley from Tsargrad only two days ago? Have done with it all, I say. The boy lies as all boys lie. When I spoke of examining him it was only in jest. In Heaven's name, take him away and let us come back to the business of men."

The Duke sank back in his place again, but a murmuring went around the hall. It is probable that the greater number there agreed with Phokas, for they came out of the East and did not like the Poles. But Michael held his peace, for he saw that the thrust had gone home. It was positive now that the Duke knew nothing of the happening in Lvov, and that Phokas was quite anxious that he should not know.

At length the Duke said: "You speak strange words, and there is something in them that seems to ring true. But I know that in this matter you must be mistaken, for Phokas has but come here direct from the capital city, and there is no dwarf in this camp. If there has been such an attempt upon the life of your king, I am indeed sorry, but the attack has not come from here. But on this I will question you again on the morrow for I fear lest some such attack as this should be laid to my door."

The guards led the boy away, but as he passed Phokas he could see that the astrologer's brow was heavy with moisture—there was in his own heart a triumphant beating that he had gone through this trial without exposing his father's plans and without weakening before questions. And he felt as well, though this without much triumph for he had made a dangerous enemy, that he had saved himself from persecution at the hands of Phokas by his quick attack. And when he came back to the room in which he was held prisoner he sat for a time with his head in his hands, thinking steadily and earnestly.

[ 58 ]

# THE DEN OF THE LION

Phokas then, with the dwarf—and where could the dwarf be?
—was playing another game besides that of aiding Duke Lev and
attempting to gain him power. Was his astrology genuine, or
was he merely using it to cloak some design of his own? And
above all what was the Golden Star of Halich?

# CHAPTER V

## THE VAULTED WAY

HE had slept through the night and part of the morning when the servant came in with food. A hot and savory dish it proved to be, for the Duke had given orders that he was to be well treated, and the servant seemed in his manner well-disposed, as toward a guest rather than a prisoner. However, the bars were still in place. He finished the meal and ran toward the casement openings, and looking out through them saw the river below and the long stretch of ruined streets and fertile fields and peasants' huts clear over to the ridge above the Tchev river.

For a moment the beauty of the scene drove all thoughts from his mind; in utter surrender to the spell of the sunlight outside he leaned against the wall and drank in the heat and light. Then as the spell lessened and the reality of the world about came to him more strongly, his thoughts leaped to one idea—and that idea, escape.

He rushed quickly to the barred gate. Outside along the corridor and all through the building was a very pandemonium of crashing hammers and cries and shouts of workmen renovating the old castle. Now and then a party of them came by, carrying stone or board or instruments of building; they were merry too, singing and joking, and even nodding at the prisoner, for they were receiving good wages for their efforts. The Duke was not one to raise workmen by levy and keep them at it by force; he wanted good work and he was willing to pay for it.

# THE VAULTED WAY

Turning back to his room, with eyes intent upon the floor, which had not yet received much attention from the workmen, Michael walked about kicking at the loose boards with his foot. Beneath these boards he found heavy cross-pieces which evidently were the supports of the ceiling in the chamber below. He worked his way about the room trying a board here and there with his foot, until he came to the corner where his bed stood. There a loose board suddenly tilted forward as he prodded it, and slid ahead and then down out of sight. In a flash he was down on his hands and knees by the side of the bed; all at once he began to tremble. A second board followed the first and came to rest a short distance beyond his reach, down almost out of sight. Pushing the bed away from the wall, he dislodged a third and a fourth, reached in an arm, and felt the chill of cold stone. He thrust his feet into the aperture, stood upon the stone surface and reached down again with his hands. Another stone, lower, but similar to the first.

Then there was a third, then a fourth—he was through the opening clear to the waist. He had discovered a flight of stairs!

But suddenly fearful lest the servant should return he leaped back to the flooring and replaced the boards, covering the place well over with the bed, so that it seemed as before. Then he sat down upon the bed and began to think.

There might be escape here. The power of hope was so mighty that for a moment he did not think of difficulties. They came quickly, however; the stairs might lead nowhere in particular, they might end in some corridor now blocked up; but hope whispered that they went to some underground passage which led out into the air; once there, he knew the way to the village, and across the bridge to Bolshov. It was a chance well worth the taking. But it was not possible in day-time—and then again what chance had he at night? No lights would be possible and

[ 61 ]

unless there was an opening not far distant, then he must grope his way in pitchy darkness. Still, it was a chance.

From the noon meal and from the evening meal he saved what food he could. This he tucked away in his jacket. For water he must trust to luck.

As night fell, huge torches of pine knots were placed along the corridor walls in sockets; they threw smoky shadows along the corridor, and filled the room with a rather pleasant odor of burning pitch. The light came fitfully, playing about the room brightly when the torches blazed up, and a few seconds later plunging it into shadows as the zest of the blaze died down. Michael had rather expected that he would be called into the presence of the Duke some time during the day or night, but evidently the ducal court was too busy with newer things to bother with him, or else the Duke had obtained what he wished.

And so he sat alone as the night fell.

How late it was when he removed the boards from the stairway he did not know. While waiting for the castle to resolve itself into silence, for all to retire save here and there a guard with a clanking sword who would call the hours during the night, he had fallen into a light sleep. But awaking in alarm lest the night had passed, he worked with furious fingers at the loosened boards and soon had them pushed out of place. As he slipped through the opening on to the stairway, he thought at first of shoving the boards back again over his head in order to mislead pursuers if his escape was noted, but finally decided simply to go down a few steps and work the bed back into its place over the aperture. Then, in the dimly lighted room, his absence would not be noted quickly.

This done, he drew in his belt and began the descent. He counted twelve steps, fifteen, twenty, and still the course was down and down. Fumbling with his hands at both sides, for the stairway was cut through solid rock, he now began to feel that the side walls were covered with moss, and the dry feeling that had been in the air when he started was changing to dampness and chill. Then he lost count of the stairs but he continued to descend. The going was slower because of his uncertainty now as to where the bottom might lie, and he finally went gingerly from step to step, making sure each time that there was a stone beneath and not the edge of some precipice or a rushing underground river.

The end came suddenly. At a period in the descent when he had begun to expect that the stairway would never end, his advancing foot went down no farther, but slid along a damp surface. He caught the other foot up to it, and edged ahead. He took at least two steps before he was fully convinced that he had reached the bottom. Then, turning, he felt the walls with his hands. To the right there was sheer rock; directly in front was rock; to the left there was emptiness, and in this direction he must go. At first in fear of plunging unexpectedly down some terrible abyss he crawled along on his hands and knees, but the rock beneath was damp and disagreeable, so he resumed his upright position to advance step by step, slowly.

Once he rested and measured the width of the passage and its height; he could easily back against one wall and touch the other with outstretched hand. The roof he could not reach, but he could tell that it was not high because of the distance from the ground at which the upper portions of the sides commenced to curve, to meet above his head in a kind of barrel roof. As he figured out directions from the position of the stairway, the passageway ran from southwest to northeast; in other words in the direction of the village and the bridge.

How far he went in this manner he could not tell; it was a veritable snail's pace, labored, painful, and fearful, for should he meet anyone in that passage there would not be room for them to pass each other, and death would probably be the portion of one. But after he had traveled for what seemed to him nearly half a lifetime, he suddenly paused and his heart began to knock at his ribs.

There was a light ahead! It was a small light, to be sure, but since it was a light it betokened the presence of other people, and it was people above all things that he wished to avoid. So crouching in order to swing quickly and retreat if there came the sign of a human being, he studied the little flicker that might mean anything. . . . The light was red . . . reminded him of something . . . puzzled him for a moment, and the truth came. It was surely the light of a shrine, probably a small lamp filled with precious oil. But what could be the use of a shrine here? Had the steps led to a subterranean church? He crept a little closer and saw that the vault he was in widened considerably; closer yet to the light he went, listening intently, gazing ahead, with all his faculties at their keenest. All at once the corridor ended; it merged with a huge vault that in turn extended on out of his sight. There was a vaulted ceiling, a line of columns; to one of these columns he crept and looked about—then in a flash everything was clear.

He was in a crypt under the Cathedral. The red light was burning before a shrine at some tomb, and now in the faint light thrown by the lamp he could discern other tombs. Curiously enough, though for that matter naturally enough, he felt no fear, for the dead never injure a living thing, and one only prays for the repose of their souls. Indeed in a world that was full of hostile forces—man against man—the peace of a crypt was a solace. In the faint light he could see that the crypt possessed a majesty and a grandeur; huge sepulchers of stone with effigied warriors and ladies upon them were ranged about in niches in the wall or rested on pillars or upon thick supports. Here then, lay the

THE VAULTED WAY

dukes of old Halich and their druzinas or courtly followings;
here lay the old bishops and the great folk of old.   For years
this crypt had been neglected, but when Duke Lev returned he
had taken pains to set this place in order, as indeed he was bringing order everywhere, and it was at his command that the light
was kept burning at the shrine.

From his place behind a pillar Michael began to plan the next
steps of his journey.   He could no doubt find a passageway, here,
up to the church and from there he might pass out and follow
along the River Lukiev.   But on the other hand such a course
would be fraught with danger since there must be guards and men
of the Duke's retinue on duty in the court outside the church; for
the church was but a part of the great ducal palace, and the towers
which flanked the court outside were full of armed men. . . .
Perhaps, on the farther side of the crypt, there was a continuation
of the passageway he had followed; it was the thing to search
for at any rate.   He was about to cross, cautiously, fearing lest
someone should come to fill the lamp, when there came to his ears
the sound of footsteps—someone was coming down a stairway at
the far end of the crypt.

In a flash the boy threw himself behind a huge sarcophagus that
jutted out from the wall at right angles, not far from the place
where he had stood by the pillar.   It was perfect protection from
an approach from the opposite end of the crypt; it was no protection at all should the person continue along toward the vaulted
way by which he had entered, and realizing this Michael huddled
up in the corner trembling and praying that the newcomer had
an errand in the other end of the crypt.

On—on—on—the footsteps came.   Nearer—nearer—nearer
—Michael nearly shrieked, for it seemed as if at the next moment
the man would pass his hiding place and spy him at once.   But
at a distance of about ten feet from the boy he stopped.

[ 65 ]

# THE GOLDEN STAR OF HALICH

There was a long silence.  The other was waiting or searching for something; suddenly he struck a sarcophagus a sharp blow
with a stick he carried.  Michael, crouching, peered around the
farther end of the tomb that protected him, and saw to his horror
that the newcomer was tall and clad in white—the astrologer—and
then to his further horror he saw a squat head suddenly raise
itself from the sarcophagus which the astrologer had struck!
A leering face appeared, followed by rounded shoulders, mis-
shapen, though huge and muscular—one leg was thrown over the
edge of a tomb which had ceased to be a resting place for the dead
scores of years before—a leg clad in black, the other leg following
quickly, and the dwarf who had thrown the dagger at King Kazimir emerged wholly from empty space and slid down to the floor!
He was clad in black as before, a cap like the skull cap of a poor
scholar fitting down close about his head.

"Something to eat," he muttered, sullenly.

The astrologer handed him a small bundle which contained food.
"Quietly, or someone will hear us."

"Well enough for you to say that," growled the other in a
surly tone.  "Here I've been in this hole for twenty-four hours
while you sat in the palace overhead and troubled yourself not at
all about me.  How much longer must I stay here?"

"Have patience.  It will be only two days longer."

"Two days with these ghosts?  I tell you I won't."

"You must.  The Master himself will be here then."

There was silence for a while.  Then the dwarf said: "Phokas,
have you any news?"

"Yes.  More galleys have come in today and more are due
tomorrow."

"Then why must I stay here?  Can't you say that I came with
the new arrivals?"

"You would be in peril of your life. . . . Do you remember that young brat that caused you to miss your aim in Lvov?"

"Could I forget?"

"Well. He is here. . . . A prisoner. And he has told the Duke that an attempt was made upon the King of Poland by you."

"By me?" Hungry as he was, the dwarf stopped eating and stared at Phokas, his jaw dropping.

"Yes. He described you. I laughed the matter off, but if you were to show yourself, then the Duke would know that the boy's story was true."

Silence again. "But could I not come out if I did not come near the castle?"

"No. I tell you it is impossible. We were sent here to play our parts. The Emperor is like this Duke here, afraid of shedding any blood. He thought you came merely as my servant, not knowing that the nobles in Tsargrad sent you to remove Kazimir from our path; what you will answer to them, I don't know. I risked my life to see it through, but you let a boy get in your way."

"I couldn't help that."

"No. And no one knows but that we shall have Poles upon our necks before the other Greeks arrive. The boy was coming here with a party of spying Poles when he was captured."

"Where is he?" The expression in the dwarf's eye boded no good to Michael.

"In one of the unfinished rooms. I believe that we can attend to him later."

The dwarf finished his meal. "How go things here?"

"One never knows. To tell the truth the whole affair seems a gigantic piece of folly to me now. We come here from Tsargrad as part of a conspiracy to put the Emperor back on his throne; to accomplish that and drive out the Turks we must have allies. And

[ 67 ]

so the nobles who believe in our Emperor persuade the Tartars to join with them; they send envoys to the Lithuanians, the Polovtsy tribe, and other wanderers on the steppe. Then it so happens that the Khan of the Tartars has not yet chosen the grand duke of the Russias, whether it is to be Dimitri of Suzdal or Dimitri of Moskva. It seems certain, however, that Dimitri of Suzdal will be put in power by the Tartars, and then that will throw to our forces hundreds of thousands of the men of Rus—the best warriors in the world."

"But tell me again—where does this Duke Lev of Halich enter into the matter?"

"That is the center of the plot; all these rulers are to be established in their own principalities; this Duke will be the ruler of Halich, which will have its old boundaries, Olgerd will rule Lithuania, our Emperor the Eastern Roman Empire, and Dimitri of Suzdal will rule the Russias; the Tartars will be in the confederation and will join with us all to drive back the Turks from the lands of the Eastern Roman Empire."

"But what holds all these together?"

Phokas hesitated, looked about, and then lowered his voice. "Do you not know that?"

The dwarf shook his head.

"Do you not know that there is a story all through the East that in a great day the nations will be led by a Star?"

"A Star?"

"Yes, and for many years it has gone about that the Star is the Golden Star of Halich. It is for this that the Tartars have come; also the Lithuanians, the Polovtsy, and the other tribes. For under the Golden Star of Halich it is said that all these nations will unite and rule the world."

"Have you seen this Star then?"

"That I may not say."

The dwarf leaned back for support against a tomb. "Had I known this, I should not have come."

"Why?"

"To put such trust in a legend, to think that Tartars and Greeks and men of Rus will unite because of a Star. . . . I shall go back with the galleys as soon as I can."

"You cannot. You are pledged to stay here." Then suddenly changing his tone, the astrologer spoke in friendly confidence. "I told you all this tonight in order that you might understand what we are doing here. It may be a fool's errand and again it may not. For my part in this business is to keep the party of nobles in Tsargrad informed of all that is going on; to delude this Lion Duke into thinking that the stars are fighting for him (instead of for us); and if the plan succeeds, of which sometimes I have grave doubts, then we will both be rich beyond our dreams. However, if the plot fails, and if there comes trouble, as I half expect, I am already prepared. You and I will be safe—come what may to the others."

"How?"

"I have arranged fire tubes in the towers that guard the Cathedral and the court. These are long barrels of iron that will hurl stones; I think I have spoken to you of this. The Tartars know the substance I use in them, and the Chinese as well, though neither have used them in this form. In Germany these have been used to drive a foe from a city; Roger Bacon, our brother in the craft in England, has already demonstrated the power of this fire; in France and at Florence these tubes have been used for defence. Filled with this substance that explodes, and with stones and pieces of metal in the tube, a very storm of stone and iron can be hurled upon an invading force. It burns more rapidly than our own Greek Fire, though it is allied to that in its composition."

"How many of these tubes have you?"

"A large number in each tower, and in the next two days I shall arrange to have you go up to the towers and learn how to set off the tubes.  If worst came to worst, you could man one tower and I the other until an enemy was routed, and then we could make the boats and escape."

They spoke together for a half-hour longer at least, and then the astrologer departed cautiously in the way that he had come. The dwarf, after watching him go, had jumped back into his sarcophagus and remained there so quietly that Michael, all a-tremble at what he had heard, thought that he must have gone to sleep.  The boy waited, however, for at least an hour more before stirring.

Then he rose to his feet, surveyed the crypt as far as he could see—dropped to his knees again and started to crawl in the direction in which the astrologer had gone.

He was just opposite the red light, which flickered with a curious draft of air, when suddenly the dwarf's head popped out of the sarcophagus where he had been hiding.  He had evidently not gone to sleep.  In reality he was planning out some way to spend his two days in some place other than the tomb, when the very slight noise made by the boy in creeping along came to his ears.  In alarm he looked out to see who was there.  At first the sight of Michael was like the sight of something unreal; the surprise of it paralyzed his faculties; he gazed straight at Michael and Michael gazed straight at him.

Michael let out an exclamation, the dwarf screamed, and then the boy flung himself to his feet and was off toward the farther end of the crypt.  But the dwarf, coming to his senses in a flash, and seconding his observation with the words of the astrologer, realized that the boy who had frustrated him in Lvov was there, within a stone's throw almost.  In an instant he had slipped to the floor and had his knife in his hand.

The entrance to the crypt from the north side was a rounded arch, so low that a man must lower his head in order to pass through. Michael dodged just in time to save himself from dashing out his brains against it, and as he dodged, something struck the arch above his head with a crash and a ring of steel, and fell at his feet. It was a dagger with a fairly long handle, hurled by the dwarf. He seized it up eagerly, and without slackening his speed either, for his own weapons had been taken away by the Tartars; then he dashed ahead into the corridor which ran in the opposite direction from the vaulted way through which he had entered the crypt.

Suddenly light streamed down from above; there was a double flight of stairs at this point, leading up on both the right and the left sides. Hesitating, he knew not which to take, glancing first to the one and then to the other and finally choosing neither —only hurling himself ahead into the darkness, into a continuation of the vault. It was fortunate that he did so, too, for it was just a fraction of a second later that the dwarf dashed into the space at the foot of the stairs; he, too, hesitated for an instant, and then flew up the stairs to the right, judging that the boy would dash for liberty that way. But at the head of the stairs he saw his mistake; a lamp there, burning before a shrine, threw its light upon doors shut and bolted. Descending rapidly he darted into the dark vault but made slow progress since it was as black as the deepest night, and he was compelled to go forward at little faster than a walking pace, with his hands held out in front of him lest he should bump against some object in the dark.

Not so with Michael, however. Desperation drove his feet ahead at high speed. Had the vault ended in some pit, or even had there been, anywhere along the stone flooring, dislodged blocks or pieces fallen from the roof, he might have been thrown forward with a terrible impact. But as luck would have it, the passageway was smooth and straight; and the flooring, though slippery in places, was solid and whole. Once he thought that far back he could hear someone shouting, and once something brushing against his face nearly paralyzed him with shock and surprise; the flutter of wings that followed the collision convinced him that a bat had whirled against his face. He had no time, however, to think of such a trifle, once he had ascertained that it was a trifle.

As he ran desperately along, the passage began to dip, and he felt himself sliding as if toward some level. Then all at once the downward direction ceased—it was damp, and drops of water came upon his face. There was no time, however, to indulge in the lesser fear, for the dwarf was somewhere behind and a meeting with him probably meant death; and if he encountered an underground river, drowning in it was preferable to meeting the deformed monster in the dark, with his knives.

There was no rush of water, however, to mark a stream, though the dripping all about increased as he went on; figuring as nearly as he could the distance from the castle and Cathedral to the vault, and the distance he had traveled, it seemed as if he must be near the edge of Krylos Hill. Then it came to him that he had reached the edge of the hill and was under the River Lukiev. He pushed ahead quickly and after a time the vault grew dry again. Then suddenly as one of the most welcome sights he had ever seen, a whole galaxy of stars burst upon his vision and he knew that he was near the end of the passage.

Approaching the exit, he turned about and listened; there was no sound behind him; evidently the dwarf had given up the pursuit. Then he walked out into the air and saw that he was near the road by which he had been brought in by the Tartars on the preceding day. Two large trees concealed the exit.

"For the moment I am safe," he thought, and began to follow

*Michael's Escape from the Dwarf*

THE VAULTED WAY

the road in the direction of the village, not traversing the worn-
down part but keeping well at the edge near the underbrush where
he could leap into concealment at a minute's notice.  It was a
glorious night, the air was clear and the stars were of gold.  In
no place in the world are the Heavens more beautiful than in the
Red Land, Galicia and Podolia; the atmosphere here is like a
glass which intensifies human sight, and the stars shine so brightly
that any traveler may find his way by means of them.  And to
the boy who had been traveling in utter darkness the starlight was
of an almost unbelievable brilliancy.

He had intended at the beginning to follow his original plan
and push on to the village which lay near the bridge, but after he
had gone about two miles he looked ahead and saw a red glow arising over the meadows that lay between him and the village.  Out
there on the steppe a peasant cottage was burning; the glow increased, changed from red to yellow and then back to red again;
as the flames leaped from the thatch of the roof to the barns and
outhouses, the fire began to ascend in a giant whirl, caught up by
a cloud of dark smoke which hid the pointed tongue of flame.

"It lies right in my path," he thought.

Then he remembered that the whole district was full of wild
tribes from the steppes, Tartars, and others, and he reasoned that
this was merely an incident in the gathering of troops, when a
body of them had probably gotten out of control.  It certainly
would not do to continue his journey in that direction; he would
but strike into the very heart of a raiding party.

So he turned off to the left and soon found the road by which
the Tartars had led him into the city.  He skirted the edge of
this for a mile or more, when the sky began to turn gray and the
birds began to sing.

"Daylight.  This will never do," he said to himself.  And as
the sun rose behind him he looked about for shelter; there it was

not far from the road, a ruined Tserkiev with a portion of some holy picture still showing stained and broken over the portal arch. He went slowly and cautiously among the roofless pillars and crumbling walls, until at length he came to a room that had once been a robing room for priests just by the side of an altar. The roof was not wholly gone here, and the floor was free from ruins; it was sheltered and offered a place for concealment. He threw himself upon the floor and closed his eyes. In a few minutes he was fast asleep.

# CHAPTER VI

## A COMPANION IN FLIGHT

THE sun, shifting about into the west, in mid-afternoon cast his rays suddenly into the boy's eyes and brought him back to consciousness with a start. He rubbed his eyes, leaped to his feet, and stretched his muscles in the pleasant gleam, then as the thoughts of his escape came to him one by one, he leaned against the broken wall and reviewed what he had accomplished. He had escaped from the castle, that was a fact for satisfaction—he had come out under the very eyes of the dwarf almost, and he had found a refuge in this ruined Tserkiev. And yet, on the other side of the matter, he had been obliged to desert the main road, which led to the bridge across the Dniester and thence to Bolshov and his father, because of the sight of a burning peasant cottage which was undoubtedly fired by the Tartars.

He took some food from inside his jacket and munched it; water would have gone well with it, but there seemed to be none within immediate reach. He would have to go back to the Lukiev river perhaps. But that was the way he had planned to go—he must make sure that the Tartars were not in the village before he tried to reach the bridge. On the other hand he might go around the village by continuing on the road by which he had come here, crossing the Tchev river at the ford and watching for some craft in which to cross the Dniester. If the water were not too swift it might be possible to swim, or else if a peasant or a fisherman had a boat by the water's edge, he could persuade him with promise of future reward to row him across to the north bank, whence he could easily make his way to Bolshov.

But what a thing was thirst! The bread he had eaten only intensified his longing for water a thousandfold. Would it not be possible to retrace his steps to the Lukiev river immediately, and quench the thirst? Then he could hide in the high bushes by the bank until nightfall, and go on straight to the village. He reached this actual determination and in a trice had jumped up and made his way cautiously out to the ruins of the arched door that faced the road; he thrust his head through the opening. The coast was clear to the west, and to the east as well—no, there was a cloud of dust rising in the road eastward from the ruined Tserkiev, down toward the little bridge that spanned the Lukiev. For a moment he kept his eyes upon this cloud to determine the nature of it and the direction, and then all at once he saw that it was approaching. Horsemen no doubt, and riding rapidly, for as the cloud came nearer he saw that it was as dense as is the dust that is thrown up by horses galloping at their fastest.

He squatted behind the nearest pillar and watched.

All at once out of the dust appeared a horse, a small brown horse, dashing violently up the slope with terrific clatter; then out of the flying particles appeared another horse, a gray—and it, too, was being urged ahead as fast as it could go.

At first he could not see who the riders were, for the distance was great and the cloud of dust befuddled one's vision; but before he discerned them, he saw in a moment that the person on the gray was pursuing desperately the person on the brown. And now the sun's rays fell upon the rider in the rear and were reflected on the instant from something bright that was held in the rider's hand—it was a sword—this Michael could make out, a long curved sword, and it flashed vigorously in the sun. They were coming nearer and nearer and he saw that the wielder of the sword was a short man, dark-faced, with dark hair and dark beard.

But the person on the brown!  He had been so much occupied with the sight of the man that he had not scrutinized the one who was being pursued; but as his eye fell upon that one, he leaped from his place of concealment and rushed out to the edge of the road, forgetting his thirst, his caution, his purpose of remaining unseen.  For the person who rode the brown horse was a girl, clad in a velvet riding suit—her hair streaming out on the wind like pure gold caught the glint of the afternoon sun.  And the girl was Katerina, the girl with whom he had talked in the Tsigan camp, the girl who had called upon him for aid.

How long the flight and pursuit had gone on Michael had no way of knowing, but it was evident that it was about to end here; and the man who followed, a Poloviets, member of one of the tribes of the steppe nearly exterminated in the Tartar wars and practically absorbed by the Nogais, had in his bearing the evident intention of violence.

With the dexterity of those who have lived in the saddle all their lives, he dashed swiftly alongside the girl rider and seized her horse's rein with his left hand; slowing gradually he cut down the speed of the other horse by a series of cruel tugs at the animal's tender mouth.  The girl's horse reared and plunged, stopped momentarily, and like a flash the dweller of the steppe had snatched her out of her saddle and flung her across his own, lengthwise like a roll of carpet; with a dig of his own spurs, he swung about, and in the next instant would have been away.

But Michael had already reached the place where the rider had taken Katerina; his heart was thundering like a great river, and the blood was surging into his temples.  Though a mere boy he felt himself in the grip of a huge emotion of rage, and in no way mindful of his own safety threw himself in wild desperation at the man on the horse.   Leaping wildly up to the saddle almost, and catching the rider by the waist, he pulled at him with all the force that he could summon.   But the Poloviets, still clinging to his prize, released the horse's reins and reached for the curved sword which he had hung upon his saddle-hook just as he had leaned forward to snatch the girl from her horse.   Michael saw the gesture, realized his own impotence—he could not dislodge the rider and the next minute the sword would descend upon him. Desperately, insane almost with fury and the combat, the boy snatched up from his jacket the knife which the dwarf had thrown at him in the vault—he clung tight with his left arm, and drove the knife blade with all his force into the rider's shoulder.

With a piercing scream the Poloviets released the girl from his grasp.   She fell forward and slipped to the ground unhurt.   Then mindful of nothing but the pain in his shoulder he reached for the handle of the knife to dislodge it if possible, and as he reached, Michael closed tight with both arms over his neck.   They hung then for a moment in mid-air, the horse plunging and neighing and biting, and as the blood began to stain the brigand's coat he weakened and fell, the boy still clinging to him, and on top; one foot came out of the stirrup, the other remained in place, and the horse, suddenly darting off, dragged them for a short distance until, fortunately for both, the saddle girth snapped and they lay sprawling on the ground.

Michael at length rose up. . . .   The other did not. . . . His chest was heaving as he took in great gulps of air, though he was only half conscious, stunned by the fall and the loss of blood. The knife had been dislodged by the fall and was beside him on the ground.   The boy took it up.

And now Katerina had grasped his hand, her eyes blazing with gratitude.   "Michael," she exclaimed, "Michael," and could say no more for the excitement that was upon her.

*Katerina Rescued from the Poloviets*

(Border from Armenian Gospel of 1198)

# A COMPANION IN FLIGHT

But he looked back, down the road, and what he saw set his heart to leaping again. "See," he cried, "there are others . . . See." He pointed toward the village.

In the midst of a cloud of flying dust, a troop of riders, Polovtsy probably like the man on the ground beside them, were approaching up the road. Their dark garments and silver ornaments offered a striking contrast.

"Quick. On the horse." He brought the brown horse back from the side of the road where it had wandered after the girl had been snatched from its back.

"You must come as well," she exclaimed as she mounted; he looked for a moment after the flying gray of the Poloviets but it was too far to be captured.

"Come." He glanced at the tower of the church of St. Pantalemon, off on a roadway to the right.

"We will seek refuge there." He leaped up behind her on the horse's back and pointed the way. In a moment they were galloping.

The road turned, rose sharply, then crossed the summit of a hill before plunging down into a hollow. Then it rose again, and they were on the ridge above the River Tchev.

"How did you come here? I thought you were a prisoner," she said breathlessly as they were speeding along.

"I was. I escaped." Then suddenly the curious truth of the situation came upon him. "I am your enemy," he exclaimed, smiling. "Will you give me up?"

"How could I?" She looked back at him seriously. "When you saved my life from that man?"

"Would he have killed you?"

"Michael, I do not know. That is the truth of it. I thought that all these people were allies of my father, and therefore friendly to me. But I find it different."

[ 83 ]

"What can it be then?" he asked. "Do you think they knew who you were?"

"I think they did."

"Then what does it mean? Troops out on an expedition such as this do not waste their time trying to capture some harmless person. It might have been ransom, and yet that was not possible if they knew that you were the daughter of the Duke."

The horse came to a hill strewn with rocks, and for a few minutes both were occupied in clinging to their places. "I can see nothing of the pursuers," said Michael looking about. "I think that they went straight up the road instead of turning off to the right as we did. There is a bend in the road just below the place where it branches and we were well hidden from their sight."

A bell-tower, partly in ruins, loomed before them. Michael stopped the horse and dismounted. "There is an old church here where we can probably find a hiding place," he continued. "Jump to earth and I will take the horse to some place where he cannot be found. It would be madness to return to the main road now, but when it is dark we can creep along by the side path and perhaps light upon the highway to Krylos. Or perhaps by that time your father will be out searching for you with a party of his men."

"I think that likely," she answered, and leaped to the ground.

He climbed back into the saddle and rode on ahead to a place where the road turned down over a hill on its way to the meadow lands, but he did not follow that turning; instead, he got down from the saddle and led the horse on through a clump of trees to the right of the traveled way. There was a spring here and both he and the horse drank greedily of the sweet, cold waters. Then following the little brook for a short distance he tethered the horse in a little clump of trees.

# A COMPANION IN FLIGHT

With his eye always upon the tower of the church, he circled back to the left of the road by which he had come. The ground was at first smooth, then came piles of stones, then a high wall that was perhaps part of the ramparts of the old city, perhaps a protection of the village that later grew up around the church, or perhaps a wall protecting the church itself. From its top he looked back down upon the River Dniester, and at the blonie or pastures lying at his feet; these were the pastures above the Bloody Ford, so called because in early wars with the Hungarians the slaughter had been so great that the river ran red with blood. Over beyond were the flats of Batiuchov, where once a sudden rise in the river had overtaken and drowned three hundred merchants with their wagons and cargoes of salt which they were bringing to Halich for export to Kiev and Tsargrad.

A flying leap and he was in the church yard. "Katerina, Katerina," he called aloud, circling the church from right to left for luck as he hastened to the main portal. And as he ran there came into his head a swift image of the girl; it was but a fleeting realization, but it was keen and real. She like a picture, with her blue eyes and her golden hair like the halo of a saint; her very beauty put his thoughts upon a new plane of living, and at that instant he came upon her, the afternoon sun upon her face and hair. She was standing before the marvelous west portal of the church, looking for all the world like an image that had just flown down from the great colored picture above the entrance.

In early days the Tserkiev of St. Pantalemon was but little less gorgeous than the Cathedral of Our Mother of God on Krylos Hill. It stood in the center of a thickly populated district which was almost a grod in itself, and indeed some of the early chroniclers believed that the very ancient city of Halich stood here or not far away. It was built in true Greek form, not like the more showy buildings of eastern Rus. It had no rounded domes nor high curved arches—it was the simple Byzantine at its best. Its central tower rose high and octagonal, with long windows in each side, and at the summit rose a Greek cross above a modest dome.   Two entrances, the main portal on the west, and the second portal on the south, admitted the worshipers to a richly decorated nave; above the portal were Biblical scenes done in mosaics.   At the head of the nave were three apses, the central apse hidden by the rich ikonostasis, or wooden partition-screen, and housing the main altar.

He took her hand and they entered the church together.   "We had better remain here until it is dark," he said.

Had there been in men's hearts at all times in all ages a love and a respect for great works of art, what a world of beauty there would be today.   Once this church had been a marvel, and even now in the fourteenth century there were many evidences of that beauty.   Around the walls, about fifteen feet from the ground, were rounded niches, where once had been delineated in mosaics or other form pictures from the life of Our Lord or the Saints; the niches were wide at the bottom, with a shelf perhaps five feet deep, but narrower where the converging side and back walls formed the top, about six feet above the shelf ledge.   In some of the niches were still the remains of the old pictures, some in bas-relief, with surface extended so that the figures seemed alive. There were splotched representations of the Three Kings kneeling before the Infant Christ, St. Stefan stoned to death, St. Basil, St. Olga, and others.

"Look," exclaimed Katerina suddenly, pointing up at the niches flooded by the instreaming sunlight, "how like life those people seem when the sun touches them. . . .   Would that I might have seen these pictures before they were broken."

"It was done in the wars," he said.

"Michael."   She caught at his arm.   "Why is it that men are always at war? It means broken hearts, broken homes, broken churches. . . . I somehow feel that I may see such a war here. . . . Even that I may be the cause of war."

"You? The cause of war?" he smiled down at her.

"Yes," she answered soberly. "And do not smile. You know I told you that day when I first saw you that there was something about my coming to Halich that I did not understand? Well, I am sorry from the bottom of my heart that I came. . . . Yet I do love my father, and I know that he loves me. . . . He is noble, great, kind. But there is something in him that even I fear. It is something that I do not understand. Some ambition perhaps. He dreams of becoming what his ancestors were, of becoming Duke of Halich, and the ruler of all the lands about."

"I know."

"You do? I do not see how you could know, but there is mystery upon mystery in all this. Though if you know, perhaps you know my part in this? No? I knew you did not, otherwise you would not have smiled a moment ago. I am a part of all this, Michael, though how I do not understand. I am proud of my father that he seeks to rule the boyars once more, though perhaps the boyars are not what they were once. But I wish that I had never come. They are preparing strange parts for me in this plan; men of the armies allied with my father's give me strange glances, sometimes even bowing before me though I am but yet new among them."

The boy was silent, struggling with the desire to tell her all that he had heard in the crypt, but he did not, fearing lest it should confuse her, but instead asked her the question that had been on his mind all afternoon.

"Whence had you come this afternoon when I first saw you pursued by the horseman?"

"From the village. They told me at the castle not to ride far;

indeed I think my father would have forbidden me to leave the place, but he was not about today and I was wearying for some exercise. No one saw me when the horse was bridled except the guard at the lower gate, which I think they call the Brama Halitska; he only saluted me and let me by."

"Where did you go?"

"Straight to the village. And there I saw the whole place closed up. Windows were barred and shutters fastened everywhere. The quietness there frightened me. It was as if all had fled before a plague. I was coming back when I saw the road full of men ahead of me; they were Polovtsy, like the man you overcame in the road; they stopped me and questioned me. It seems that they had just arrived in Halich. I could not answer them for they spoke strangely. At last I rode by leaving them talking and making signs with their hands. When I thought they were far behind I looked back. One of them was riding fast towards me; I whipped up my horse, and the man came on faster, and I knew that he was chasing me, perhaps had been sent to bring me back. Thinking that I could circle back to the castle road at a point farther to the south I turned off to the right across the little stream. It was shortly after that that you saw me," she finished.

"But do you believe that they knew you?"

"As I rode through them, I heard one man speak my name, and it seemed as if he was surprised."

"I can't think what it is all about," Michael said after a moment's pondering.

Across the blonie a peasant was calling softly to his cattle—hoy-hoy-hoy!

"What is the Golden Star of Halich?" he asked suddenly.

Her hand trembled as she took it from his arm. "How did you hear of that?"

"What have I heard else?" he asked. "It is for news of that that my father and I came to Halich. Though indeed that is the business of my King, and to no one else but you would I reveal it. . . . And then again it was Phokas who told the dwarf in the crypt of the Cathedral that the Golden Star had brought all these people here."

"*Phokas* told this to the *dwarf*, you say, in the crypt of the Cathedral? And who is Phokas, and who is the dwarf, and how did you come to be in the crypt of the Cathedral?"

And at that he told her the whole story of his escape.

"Then, Michael," she spoke slowly and deliberately, "I must confess to you that although I have heard talk of scarcely anything else since I came to Halich, I do not know what the Golden Star is. I do know that it is something about which all these people are concerned; perhaps it is some prophecy, some expected star that will shine in the Heavens above this place; perhaps it is a jewel of great value; perhaps even it is an ornament of great value such as King Koloman gave to the Princess Salomea when they were married so many years ago on Krylos Hill. But I do think that it is for this star that all these tribes of the steppe have come to Halich; it is something about which those who live in the East have had knowledge. But I do not know, and this I tell you truthfully."

"Are there many men here?" he asked.

"Yes, but not so many as there will be. They come from all the East, and even from Tsargrad which the Greeks call Byzantium and the Romans Constantinople."

The words were hardly out of her mouth when there came the sound of voices from outside, a sudden clamoring sound, of men and women talking, and even children. In alarm they looked about the church for a hiding place. The apses full of fallen rubbish, the windowed niches, the fallen ikonostasis—but as they were rushing toward the front of the building there came to their ears the sound of singing:

> *Our cities are in ruins but we want them so,*
> *As we wander o'er the Czarny Szlak;*
> *We tread the friendly earth or we ride the "roads that go"—*
> *Come and follow in the Tsigan track.*

"Tsigani," they shouted together in glad relief, and rushed out toward the side door.

Some children playing just outside thought them spirits, for they ran away shrieking. Not so the women who had been standing nearby, when they laid eyes upon Katerina. "Stasko. Stasko," they shouted.

He came running. "What do you here?" he exclaimed when he saw the girl. "And is this not the Korzets?"

"It is, Stasko. It is," she shouted. "This is Michael. I was chased by brigands, and he saved me, and we took refuge here. . . . But we are hungry, and we want to get back to the castle; perhaps you can take us."

"I would be set on my way to Bolshov," declared Michael. "My father is there. I escaped from the castle in order to return to him."

"But does the Duke know you are here?" Stasko addressed Katerina, disregarding seemingly the boy's words.

"No. That is why I would have you take us to the castle, though perhaps it would be better to set Michael upon his way."

He called the clan about him. "Suppers for all. And be ready to leave at once." Then turning to Katerina he bade her tell him the whole story. When she had finished he exclaimed: "I am sorry that we loitered here. You are in very great peril. To get you back to the Duke I must transform you both into

Tsigani immediately. Bring some garments that will fit them," he called out to a woman who stood near.

"But can I go my way?" asked Michael.

"No."

"Why not?"

"Your life would not be worth a grain of wheat. Every road, every path, every ford—indeed every bush and every tree in Halich is watched tonight and will be for many nights to come."

"Then I must go back to prison?"

"It is the only way. I am sure, though, that the Duke will be merciful to you when he learns that you have saved his daughter. It is the only way. Nothing but death lies ahead of you if you venture farther in this direction."

"But I am afraid that my father thinks me dead, though the Duke had word that he and his party rode away from Halich as if they knew that I was safe."

Stasko thought a moment. "Where is he now?"

"At Bolshov."

"That is not far. I will carry word myself."

"Good Stasko," the boy embraced him, "and tell him that many armies are gathered here. If he would rescue me he must come with a large force."

"I will," said the Tsigan. "I owe the Korzets family much."

"Heaven bless you."

Tsigan clothes were brought out for them to put on; they had retired to the church to dress themselves when suddenly there came the sound of galloping hoofs over the hill, and a large body of Polovtsy in their long black coats and astrakan caps dashed into the very middle of the Tsigan camp.

# CHAPTER VII

## THE GOLDEN STAR

MICHAEL never quite knew just how he did it. But at the first sound of Polovtsy voices outside the church he had leaped and scrambled somehow up over a heap of ruins into one of the niches in the wall of the church, and reaching out drew Katerina up beside him. The floor was fully the height of two men below, but projecting stones and beams had given him a foothold. But the speed with which it was all accomplished amazed even the boy himself when he thought of it later.

Had it only been dark then some corner of the church or the shelter of the broken ikonostasis might have made a better hiding place; or perhaps there would have been an opportunity to escape by the side door and take refuge in the moat below the old wall. But the sun seemed pausing just long enough to aid the pursuers. A dying ray, red like blood, fell through the broken roof and wall illuminating the upper portion of one side of the church; as the sun sank the ray came lower and lower and seemed about to die just as the sound of horses' hoofs crashed upon the stone pavement at the arched door.

"They will surely see us here," thought Katerina, "even though we are back from the surface of the wall." And as the sun, at that moment lighting up the remains of a picture on the wall, threw its outlines into bold relief, a plan like lightning flashed into her head. "Crouch back against your side of the wall," she directed Michael—"on your knees, and I will stand opposite."

Raising herself she stood there as close to the wall as she could get.  And as the boy, uncomprehending, fell upon his knees before her, she laid one hand upon his head and held the other close to his mouth.  And Michael glancing across the church saw instantly what was in the girl's mind; she had taken the exact posture of St. Helena in the picture over on the other wall.  She was there ministering to the poor—and before her was kneeling a man whom she was feeding.

The horses and their riders crashed into the church, riding about like mad and striking with their swords into every dark corner.  They ripped down the hanging boards of the ikonostasis, they pried off the lids of what seemed to be old tombs, they struck against the walls with their sword handles, testing to see if by chance there was a hollow place.  But in the first tumult the men had looked every way but up, and that was fortunate for the sun was still illuminating the upper part of the church, though the beam of light grew fainter every second now.

Outside the church the Tsigan leader was declaring in an excited voice to some of the Polovtsy that the boy and girl had not been seen near the camp, but no heed was paid to him at first.  In their ancient language, which Stasko understood and could reply in, they told him that they were acting on the orders of their captain, and that they were to bring the girl back with them to their camp.  She would not be harmed, they explained, but the boy must pay the penalty for wounding one of their men, and the brigand himself who had chased the girl made an angry gesture with his left arm, for his right was stiff because of his wound.  The other riders looked in all the tents, examined the packs on the backs of the horses, and satisfied themselves that there was no one behind the church or in the ditch.  Then sitting down on the ground they awaited their companions who were still ransacking the church.

[ 93 ]

These, inside the Tserkiev, however, were just about to end what seemed like a fruitless quest, when one of the Polovtsy looking upward remarked that the pictures in the church had not been so badly injured as the altars. Whereat the boy and girl, not knowing what was said, but seeing the upward glances, froze themselves into position, he, the beggar, kneeling and receiving alms—she, St. Helena, bestowing the alms upon him. On account of the depth of the shelving niche, their feet were concealed and the lower part of their bodies; from below in the fast-decreasing light one could see only the shape of a woman, in bas-relief, feeding a man kneeling before her. And it looked as if they were to pass unnoticed—though their hearts were beating so loud that it seemed as if all men could hear—when the last flicker of light from the sun threw a feeble ray through a crevice in the shattered wall directly upon Katerina's gold hair.

Michael saw it, and a prayer rushed to his lips.

One of the men below, looking up at that moment, saw it too and exclaimed loudly. Perhaps it was an expression of surprise at the sudden beauty of the sight, for the girl's head seemed surrounded by a halo of gold—the face was like the face in the gorgeous pictures of the East, the whiteness showing out against the yellow of the sun and the gold of her hair. Perhaps it was an expression of something else—they all turned, but at that moment the ray vanished; there was naught in the west now save a burst of glory where the sun had just been.

So the rest saw nothing, and while the other lingered, having a mind to investigate the beauty of the picture, there came the voice of their leader calling them outside to join the rest of the company. They wheeled out on their horses, the waiting men outside leaped up from the ground, and in a short space the troop had ridden off back in the direction of the town where their camp was.

*Like Figures in a Picture*

(Details from broken columns and capitals found on Krylos Hill)

THE GOLDEN STAR

The girl's hands trembled. "That is twice today that I thought myself near death," she said.

"And I," he said. "It was your wit that saved us."

"My arms are in agony," she exclaimed—for she had remained in her pose many minutes with arms outstretched; "indeed had they been nearer they must have seen me tremble."

"I scarce dare move now," he whispered.

"Michael . . . I shall pray to Saint Helena with thanks from this day forward."

"And I."

It was nearly dark inside the church now. Some one coming in spoke in Tsigan, and then in the language of Rus. Katerina whispered as loudly as she could, not daring to speak aloud, "Stasko. Have they gone?"

He came over and stood beneath them scarcely believing his eyes. "Where could you have hidden?" he demanded. "They must have seen you up there."

"We were like a picture," she answered. He comprehended, then clambering up over the ruins, stretched out his arms and caught her as she leaped. Michael, still clutching the bundle of clothing, which somehow he had clung to throughout, came thundering down with broken stone and plaster. "They have ridden away," said Stasko. "Put on your Tsigan clothes, and smear your faces and hands with earth."

They dressed quickly in the church and came out to the fire. So complete a transformation had the clothes wrought that neither would have known the other; Stasko, examining them, rubbed their faces and necks with some brown, paint-like substance that he had, and worked the color into the skin. And now the supper had broiled upon the fire and there was meat to eat and some kind of hot brew to drink.

After eating, Stasko gave orders quickly; there was much

hurrying about and loading of horses. No matter how disorderly the Tsigani might appear in camp, or on holidays when they betook themselves to the towns, or on the days of the fair—when they were on the march everything was in military order. Each seemed to know his place and duties. One attended to a horse, another to belongings, another counted the company and distributed the members of the clan. At length everything was finished and the fire extinguished, and the march began.

They went around behind the church and struck off for the road by which Michael had led Katerina's horse. He had already told Stasko of the horse and it had been brought to the Tsigan corral. But instead of turning right, into the woods, the company went left to the river bank, down the hill and across the long low pastures. They were some time in the descent, and once Michael looking up exclaimed:

"See. The new moon."

There it hung in the west like a sickle of silver, a gray cloud pursuing it through the Heavens.

The girl looked up at it, but the beauty of it baffled her attempt to reply.

Down the slope they went, the men in front shouting, the women calling to their children.

"They are taking us to the raft," said Michael.

"Why, I wonder?"

"I don't know. We don't want to cross if you are to find your father."

Stasko came upon them out of the darkness. "The roads are not safe," he explained. "We will go by water to the town and there look for the Duke. Should we take the road again we might meet Tartar or brigand, and not come off so fortunate as we have up yonder." He pointed up to the church, its ruined tower showing against the starry sky.

# THE GOLDEN STAR

In a moment the raft lay before them, huge at night it seemed, straining at the ropes that held it; already a dozen or more youths and men were stationed upon the edge of it ready to push off. The horses were led aboard and tied. The provisions were carried on; the women and children were placed in the middle. And now everything was in readiness and Stasko gave the word to fend. The men thrust their long poles into the shallow water at the bank and drove the raft out into the current. At first it responded but slowly to the stream, then as it gathered momentum it moved gracefully and easily out into the depths; in a few minutes it was moving downstream. The darkness was closing about them and there was only the noise of the steering poles dipped in the water and then lifted out.

Michael sat with Katerina. "See the lights," he said, pointing.

She looked. Out across the Halich plain, clear up to Krylos, was a long line of fire. As the raft swung in the current at certain angles, it seemed as if the fires were close together, but as it swung to other positions the boy and girl could see that the torches, though in a line, were far apart.

"Signals," he exclaimed. "Perhaps for us."

Below them now could be seen the houses of the new town and near these, lights were also burning, tiny lights however which seemed like pin points.

The air was a bit cool—there was a feeling that summer had almost run her course, the stars now shone like burnished gold, and the little crescent was sinking fast to the edge of the world.

"I wonder," said Katerina—"I wonder so many things."

"Such as—?"

"Well, a night like this makes me think that there are so many things greater than our little thoughts—greater than we are perhaps. . . . Men are just like the little lights we see. The Heavens and the stars and the river—all these live forever. . . .

Think of the people who have lived here. The people who have worshiped in that church where we were this afternoon. . . . The people who lived in the great city of Halich. They are all gone, yet the river flows on, and the new moon comes."

"I have thought about that," Michael broke in, "ever since I have been here. It is curious too. Here we are only a few miles from Lvov and yet it is a different world. I think it is the East."

"It is," she said. "And the new moon is part of it. It comes from the East, too. Think how the men of the East paint it on their banners."

"One would think there was nothing in the world but peace and happiness. And yet, Katerina—" he turned to her quickly and caught her hand between his—"Katerina, we may be upon the verge of a war in which our people are upon different sides. And while we must be loyal to our people, we will still be loyal to each other. Will you not swear to eternal friendship between us?"

"I swear."

On went the raft drifting idly with the current—here and there men guiding it, and all at once lifting up a song in the rhythm of the motion. Upon it the women, used to travel of all kinds, to hardship, to the roof of Heaven and never to man's roof, nursed their children or rocked them to sleep upon their breasts; the men watched the night, the river, the raft, sometimes each other. Stasko sat where he could watch the progress of the craft in the water. Down the Dniester they were floating, and "Down the Dniester," sang the Tsigani as they swung the poles to the tune. Whence came the tune they sang—from India—from Babylon—from Egypt?—a tune as ancient as man on earth, and in a language that was as sweet as any in the world. On and on and on—down the dark stream.

*Gypsy Raft on the Dniester*

(Design from broken columns found on Krylos Hill, now in Ruthenian Museum)

"My father was telling me of the ancient days on this river," said Katerina, "how the men of Rus went back and forth in their little boats until the time when the men of Tsargrad, or Byzantium as the Greeks call it, came up the river in their galleys and showed them how to make better craft. Then in those days all men were wealthy, the boyars who ruled the dukedom, the duke who was but the chosen leader of the boyars, the merchants, and even the peasants."

"But does your father hope to bring back those times?"

"I do not know. I do not know."

He had it on his lips to tell her that the land belonged now to Kazimir, who had rid it of the peoples who had harmed it, but he felt that it might hurt her, and then besides, had Kazimir rid it of the men of the East? Were they not gathering here in numbers to battle for this country, the Tartars, the Polovtsy, the Lithuanians, the men of Rus, and now even Bulgarians and Greeks? . . . He was silent, wondering how great would be the army made up of all these races.

Who was to conquer in these lands, known as the Red Land or the land of the Red Rus since the beginning of time? Would it be men from the East, and would the East penetrate the West and bring with it all that the East believed in? Or would it be that the West would conquer here and hold here her boundary line? If the East were to conquer then the civilization of the West was doomed; for the East was not the West. And he seemed to see into the future as well as the past, for a brief instant on that dark night, beneath the stars, floating on the raft down the Dniester river. This was Poland's mission in the family of nations. Her mission was to stand upon the border of East and West and keep the West for western civilization. Once the East penetrated the Red Land it was but a step to the great cities of the West, and when they fell, the rest must fall as well. He saw much—he might have seen the Poles repel the Tartars here in at least forty wars—he might have seen the Poles harry the Turks and keep them out of Europe in wars that lasted for several hundred years, wars which saved western civilization but which drained Poland of her life blood; he might have seen Sobieski at the gates of Vienna driving back the Turks—"thus far and no farther." And in later ages he might have seen the Poles on this battle front hold off the East in a new array; for the East was great and it lacked not for ideas, and when defeated in one combat it came back anew in new form. Thus had it been now for more than five hundred years, and what shall the future bring? No man knows.

He left her for a moment and joined Stasko.

"Where are you going from Halich?"

"My people go down the Dniester. I shall put back to Bolshov."

"Shall you remain in Halich overnight?"

"I shall wait only until I see the Duke. Then I am off to see your father."

"May I not go with you?"

Stasko shook his head. "That I cannot undertake."

"Why?"

"You are the prisoner of the Duke. He will treat you well after I tell him all that has happened today. We Tsigani are free to move among all people only if we do not interfere."

"Yes, but you carry news."

Stasko thought for a moment. Michael's assertion was rather staggering. "We may do that," he said. "Everyone asks the Tsigani questions and we may answer as we choose. If I do not bring news for money, then only am I free from molestation." Stasko's statement was absolutely true. On the border, the news was carried from place to place by wandering people, minstrels, peddlers—Tsigani foremost among the wanderers of the steppe. The Tsigani people occupied a place of distinct necessity in the sparsely settled regions, and although it was often complained of them that they stole and cheated, yet the sight of them was usually welcome in the days when travel was difficult and news traveled slowly. And the Tsigan might relate what he had heard among one party of men to another party, but he might not take gold for so doing. If he were paid then he became an informer, a spy, and his life was not worth a grosz if he were caught.

Thus Stasko—in the wandering life of his clan he had a distinct duty to perform; he must keep all the people among whom his people wandered friendly to himself and his clan. The Tsigan tribe wandered on a regular course, like a comet in its orbit, and if it went around a town on the course or skipped it one year, it was sure to return the next. And it was necessary to have friends in every town. Stasko performed his service excellently, knowing that no man has friends who does not give as well as take, and for his bits of news he was welcomed everywhere. Thus he could carry news to the Duke of the condition of his daughter, and on the other hand he could go to Michael's father, or to the King himself for that matter, with information desired by them. But no money must he take for so doing.

There came over Michael at this moment a temptation. It was this: to ask Stasko to take Katerina and himself to Zvinogrod, to let them live like Tsigani, free as the air. He knew that Katerina would approve of his request, but in the next moment he remembered his own duties, his very responsibilities in this troublesome affair. "Perhaps the future of the whole Eastern Provinces lies with me," he thought, and then too, there was Katerina's father. No—much as the scheme pleased him, he was forced to abandon it, and went back to the place where the girl sat watching the reflection of the bright stars in the dark water.

Suddenly the raft swung to the left. "The River Lukiev," shouted Stasko; "hold the poles close in." The raft swung back again as the poles went down. The converging current dashed against the raft but did not flood it as the men pushed the craft along quickly and deftly. And now there was looming up before them a great structure in the darkness.

"Halich bridge," shouted Stasko. "Pole in."

They sent the raft edging in toward the shore on a long slant; the river was shallow here and they were soon pushing upon the river bottom. For a time they slid softly ahead, through meadows, it seemed, for the grass was thick about them, and then finally landed upon the shore with a slight bump.

"Hold," said Stasko, leaving his post and coming across to Michael and Katerina. The men held the poles in the mud at the bottom of the stream, thus anchoring the raft to the shore. "Tie it up, and wait for me. I shall be back directly."

He leaped to the shore, reached for the hands of the boy and girl, and led them to firm ground. They followed hesitating, not knowing the land and fearing pitfalls. But all at once the dark meadow about them seemed lighter; then there spread across it a red glow; for a moment it writhed in crimson colors that twisted like serpents and then became almost as light as day.

All three of them started back in alarm—upon a height, halfway between the half-built castle on the hill above the town and the castle on Krylos, a blazing beacon was shooting red flames into the sky. It was like a burning building, a burning forest—so huge did the pyre seem at that distance; but then looking toward it they could see the shapes of men who had lighted the fire.

"That is an alarm," exclaimed Stasko. "It is for you, Katerina. Your father has sent out the signal."

He took his coat and wiped the brown grease from their faces —Michael threw himself upon the grass and rubbed his cheeks in the dew; Katerina rubbed hers with a Tsigan kerchief. Then both the boy and girl, at the direction of Stasko, threw off the disguises they wore and stood forth in their own costumes.

"Come," he cried, "before it is too late."

They went up the sloping meadow, crossed a small brook and found the main road near a peasant cottage. The light from the burning signal had been obscured for a moment while they were hidden beneath a projection of the hill, but when they came upon the road it blazed out again. And now men were about them, and there was shouting, and blowing of trumpets; the whole scene turned suddenly into a dream, and Michael was conscious that they were in the midst of hundreds and hundreds of men—some on horseback in full armor, some with pointed helmets and iron mail, others on foot in companies and in battalions, and that they all were pressing forward to the center of this group. Then all seemed suddenly to fall away, and the ground was open and empty and three figures on horseback were riding toward them.

The central figure was the Duke. In an instant he had leaped from his horse and caught the girl in his arms. And then, when his emotion had died down, he turned upon Stasko with an angry face. But a few words from Stasko changed the look and he kissed the Tsigan upon both cheeks. And in an instant he had turned toward Michael, and instead of the wrath which the boy had feared might boil over because of his flight, he felt only the grasp of the Duke's hand upon his own.

Then as this continued—this which seemed like a dream— horses were brought for them and they were riding through myriads and myriads of men, men of all races, men shouting in many tongues, and swords were uplifted and spears were waving in the air. It was like the ride of a triumphal emperor through the streets of his own capital city, when he had won a great victory. And the two men with the Duke were men of regal cast. One

THE GOLDEN STAR OF HALICH

of them, in a long black gown over which was shining armor, wore upon his head a helmet of the finest silver.  The other wore no armor, but was clad in a robe of silk upon which were embroidered lilies in all the colors of the rainbow—he was a short man with a rich, scabbarded sword at his girdle; for a helmet he wore a turban-like headpiece that in some respects made one think of a crown.  The boy fixed his gaze upon this man; there was something about his eyes that made it impossible to take his own eyes away.

But as the man looked in the other direction Michael glanced at Katerina.  She was riding a little ahead of them.  She had been given a horse which was pure white, and which although gentle was possessed of more spirit than any of the others.  As the fire streamed into the air from the hill, and as the armies pressed upon the company in the center, she stood out like a saint in gold, in a huge ikon, against a background of black.  The riding habit she wore seemed transfigured into a suit of scarlet; they had given her a short sword to carry; her hair blew loose in the wind like strands of gold.  Boy though he was, Michael knew that he might never again see such beauty in his life—never might come again such contrasts of color, as those formed by the backgrounds of darkness and the fairness of the girl who had been up to now his companion.

There was something about her that seemed suddenly imperial. She was great—she was above the race of human beings who surrounded her.  And they thought that too, and held up their swords in salute and called to her in salutation.  And as they came to the men in the armies of Rus, whose language Michael knew, he understood suddenly the great problem which had perplexed him—nay, had perplexed all the Poles and even their king, Kazimir; for this girl Katerina was the choice of peoples as one to whom they should pay reverence.  And as she went along, the roaring broke forth and swelled jubilantly louder and louder like the roar of the sea. And the words which they said were these:

"Hail, all hail, to the Golden Star of Halich!"

And by that Michael knew that Katerina was the Golden Star about which so many men had spoken; she who had been in ignorance of her position in the world, a mere girl who knew not what lay about her. And yet she rode along, proudly perhaps, perhaps frightened. The Golden Star of Halich was no jewel of cold stone; it was no ornament of lifeless metal; it was flesh and blood, and spirit—it was a fourteen-year-old girl. This was the mystery that King Kazimir had pondered upon; this was the riddle that spies had sought to solve; it was this Golden Star that Phokas had said would redeem them all; it was this Golden Star that was to come to the House of the Lion. For this Golden Star, scattered tribes had come hundreds of miles out of the steppe, galleys had sailed up the Dniester, an empire well-nigh conquered had taken heart, an extinct dynasty was awaiting a resurrection. He understood all this as a fact—what lay beneath the surface he could only surmise.

# CHAPTER VIII

## TOLD IN A TOWER

AS the whirling tumult thrust him along that night, Michael realized that the most powerful forces of the East were represented at Halich, not huge forces perhaps, for armies of great bulk could not have crossed frontiers unnoticed, but powerful groups numbering hundreds each from the land of the Tartars, from Suzdal, and perhaps Novgorod, Lithuania, Bulgaria, and Greek states to the south. Several warriors appeared to be Greeks, and as he thought of Stasko's words to his father he looked about for the Tsigan chief himself, but Stasko had slipped away long before and probably by this time was sitting on the raft looking out ahead down the Dniester and giving commands to the polemen.

Such splendor as there was about! Garments and armor a-glitter with metal like silver, some gold, precious stones in the bridles that threw back colored lights, saddles of rich leather; there were long robes, turbans, high boots, red and black—behind Katerina rode several boyars of the almost extinct line of Halich, clad in the ancient splendor of that once powerful house. Farther along were straggling commands, a few Hungarians, some Czechs, Wallachians, soldiers of fortune come together like magic at the news of new alliances.

At the Halich gate they marched through, having crossed the Lukiev by a newly constructed bridge, and entered the ducal city or grod by the old grass-grown road. In the light of flaring torches and the beacon fire still blazing on a hill over beyond, the whole mass of structures stood out in silhouette against the dark sky; the outlines were uneven, however—smooth only where the repairing had been completed, rough and jagged where roofs and towers had decayed and fallen. Straight ahead the rebuilt palace and graceful Cathedral threw their sharp, decisive realities against the nothingness behind. And as the company toiled up the approach to the Cathedral gates one of the great bells brought from Tsargrad began to sound. Clang-clang-clang-clang-clang, it sounded, and the shivering splinters of broken sound fell down about the ears of the triumphant cavalcade.

They escorted Katerina to her rooms in the palace—she looked behind once to catch a glimpse of Michael, but failed because he was cut off from view by the boyars about the Duke. Michael they escorted to his old room, but they tore off the bars at the door at the command of the Duke himself; they threw upon the floor a huge eastern rug, and set up for his use a magnificent bed. Servants came with food and wine, and waited about to see if he should ask anything further of them. But he wanted only two things now, a few minutes of solitude in which to put his thoughts together, and sleep; and though they brought rich robes for him to wear during the night, he put them on without giving much heed to them, for his wits were in a daze of wonder and there was no path through which reason could flow.

At length they left him alone; the bell ceased its clamor, and music from harps and instruments of many strings died away. The leaping red lights drooped to yellow and disappeared, and sleep came gently with soothing fingers upon his eyes.

He slept late, for sunshine was over the world when he awoke, although it did not enter his room since the windows of it faced the west. But upon his bed was the semblance of sunshine, gleaming cloth of great sumptuousness, woven with gold and silver thread—

this was the coverlid, and the cloth beneath it silk. At his home, where the humble comforts of a border *szlachta* family were enjoyed, nothing like this was known; wool blankets were used there for bedding, and the beds themselves were of pine. Here, the silks and satins and gold embroidery, the rich-woven rugs, this hardwood bed with canopy and rich veilings—these were of the East, that East whose refinements had corrupted more warriors than its armies had slain soldiers. It had been so in old days when the knights of the Polish frontier had by some stratagem entered or conquered a city of the East, when the rough life of the camp and army had been exchanged for a life of luxury and ease. When these men who had come from the West, where time is measured and divided, and each second is conquered by accomplishment— when these men of the West came suddenly face to face with the timelessness and seductive leisure of the East, it worked a change in their hearts and brought them to ill thoughts and ill deeds and ill lives.

But servants came in to help him dress. They put over his legs heavy hose, close-fitting, silken, and a richly embroidered jacket which was held together by lacing. They slipped over his head a sleeveless robe, of blue cloth with scarlet trimmings; in the presence of elders he must wear this at full length; with those of his own age he could throw it informally over the left arm, wearing it as if it were a cloak. This robe had a collar that turned up about his chin, bowl-fashion. The head-covering which was attached to the mantle hung behind when not in use. When he went out into the air he needed only to raise it over his head like a hood.

"May I go where I choose?" he asked a servant, in the language of the Rus.

"You may," the man bowed.

First however, they brought him something to eat, not the bread and water of his day of captivity, but dainty fruits and meat and the delicacies that are served at a noble's table.

Wondering at it all he wandered out into the corridor, when he had eaten, strolled along the hallway to the left, ascended a flight of stone steps and found himself at the entrance to a court that lay between that section of the house and the Cathedral. And as he was crossing the court with the intention of looking into the church, he saw a figure in white approaching from the opposite side of the court and perceived that it was Katerina.

She wore a simple robe of rich white silk, a bit heavy it seemed, caught with a girdle, sleeves puffed from the shoulder to a point below the elbow, and then close-fitting to the wrist. Her hair was braided this morning, and about her temples was a narrow gold band, embossed and colored with many flowers. The flowers were blue like the blossoms which grew everywhere in Halich.

As she approached him he saw that a subtle change had come over her features since yesterday, that there was now something of a dignity, of a seriousness, that drove away the light girlish expression that had been hers so short a time before.

But there was no change in the warmth of her feeling toward him. "Michael," she exclaimed, "Michael"—it was all that she could say at that instant.

He in turn could say nothing.

"What will come of it, Michael?" she continued.

"I cannot say," he answered.

"It hardly seems true. I . . . Michael . . . If I could only tell you all that I know. And yet, I think I will." She looked about to see if anyone was within range.

"Let us go somewhere where no one will see us."

Her eyes swept the court. "There, up in that tower," she decided.

It was the tower closest at hand which had been built as one of the two tower defences of the Cathedral. It was of stone, like the Cathedral, and was upon the left side of the entrance gate as they faced it.

An iron door at the base of this tower stood invitingly open; not hurrying, lest their movements should attract attention, they strolled in the direction of the iron door, and in a moment had entered and were toiling up the steep stairs which ran not straight up and down but around and around the interior. Once they threw themselves down upon a stone rest below a narrow window; it was but wide enough, this window, for the flight of an arrow, and in old days many an arrow had sped from that opening.

"I wonder that the towers still remain," she mused. "There have been so many wars, and most of the old buildings were torn down."

"I cannot understand that either," he answered. "Apparently Batu-Khan did not destroy the whole town, nor did he level the Cathedral walls. This tower is well built. I suppose that all the new work has been put in by your father."

"Yes. The roof and all the woodwork. The furnishings have been brought from all parts of the East. Armies of men have been at work hewing down forests, and you see how everything is being rebuilt. Most of the upper part of the castle is new—it is stone only about one-quarter of the way up; the floorings, rafters, ceilings, roofings are all new. The foundations were in good shape, and the Cathedral has been preserved almost miraculously. It is a wonder to me that the Tartars did not destroy it."

They resumed their climb again, and in a few minutes emerged at the summit of the tower. The shape of the tower was round, probably after an Arabian model—and the flooring, which was some twenty feet in diameter, was surrounded by a wall six or seven feet high. This wall was pierced by long windows for archers, and at the lower ends of these windows there had been

knocked away recently a large number of bricks. In these aper-
tures, and there were about a dozen of them on the side facing
the northwest, rested long iron tubes, curious-looking objects, with
large openings on the outer end and very small openings pierced
on the other end.

"I know what these are," exclaimed Michael, leaping forward
and examining one. "These are the fire tubes of the astrologer.
It is what I heard him talking about in the crypt."

"And what do they do?"

He explained. "My father has heard of these. He says that
they will change all warfare. You know the arbalist and cross-
bow are even now changing the style of armor that men wear in
battle."

"But will there be need of all this?" she asked.

He was silent again. What could he say? There might, and
again there might not.

"Did you tell your father what I overheard in the crypt?" he
asked.

"I had no chance. And I do not think that he would listen to
me if I did. Michael, I think that his mind is so deep in this,
that he would hear nothing that was unfavorable."

"And yet he heard what I said before the astrologer. And I
somehow feel that the astrologer fears me. Could I but see your
father I would tell him to keep the astrologer well watched, and
I would tell him to search for the dwarf in the crypt of the Cathedral and ask him a few questions. . . . Among other things
he tried to kill me . . . Katerina, I must tell your father of this.
When could I go to see him, do you think?"

She pondered for a while. "Not today, I fear, for he has gone
with his boyars on a survey of the old city. And when he returns
at night there will probably be a long council. . . . But indeed, I
believe that there is little to gain in telling him."

"But don't you see? It is for his own good. These men are unscrupulous and might stop at nothing."

"I doubt if he would listen to you now. The plot is arranged, the matters are all ready, and in a day or two the world will know what he intends."

He changed the subject for a moment. "Come up here." He pointed to a place where bricks had been built into the wall to form a staircase; going up first he drew her up to a seat beside him, on the top of the wall. The thickness of the wall, which was five or six feet, gave them a sense of safety, nevertheless they dangled their feet securely on the inside and gripped the edge of the wall with their fingers, before turning so that they could gaze at the plain below.

Built as it was upon the highest point of land in Halich, the tower perch seemed halfway up to Heaven from earth. Above them on the south rose the dome of the Cathedral—at their feet lay the rebuilt roofs of the houses adjoining the palace, and beyond them were the wooden walls leading to the Halich Gate.

From the Halich Gate the road ran like a serpent to the Lukiev where the new unpainted drawbridge spanned the stream. Men in shining armor and pointed helmets were on guard there, the sun reflecting the bubbles of the river on the bright metal. Beyond the river, and stretching away to the left, lay the Podgrodzie, or the district below the grod or castle grounds, and across it ran the roofs of peasants' houses with stone foundations, stones that were once part of the old city. Here and there were ruined buildings with trees growing up through them like grass through a sandal that has been thrown away and has lain in the snows and rains and droughts.

"If the Duke were to rebuild all of ancient Halich it would take him an hundred years," Michael thought.

Close by the junction of the castle road and the drawbridge rose the pointed dome of a Greek Tserkiev; ruins of other Tserkievs and churches, and the gaping walls of old dwors or palaces of boyars could be seen beyond. Then far to the left, perhaps three kilometers, rose high walls in the district of Biedun, the poverty-stricken district or the unfortunate district as the name implied. North of that, on the same height, overlooking the Tchev river rose the broken dome of what had once been a church as magnificent as a cathedral; and north of that, across the Kamieny Wywoz or Stony Road, rose the tower of the friendly church of St. Pantalemon where they found refuge from the brigands.

But that which was most impressive was the River Dniester, glinting at a distance like a silver mirror; one could see but little of it, yet that glimpse was thrilling. Along its banks were the blonie or pasture lands, and Michael dreamed how in its wandering course to the Black Sea it swept by cities on cliffs, cities in ruins, cities where the men of the Orient swarmed in the streets. It roared through the rapids at Yampol, and it spread out at the mouth near the old city of Tyras, now Akkerman, so that one could scarcely see across it.

"Think what this used to be," said Katerina bringing him back from the spell of river and plain.

"I have," he said.

"It thrills me when I think that this was once the land of my fathers; it thrills me in spite of myself, because, Michael, I would leave Halich this moment if I could."

"Have you thought of flight?" he asked, starting up.

"That I have. Though it seems useless, yet there is a chance. If Stasko were to return—"

"I might find him," he said. "But would you leave your father?"

"Michael—I don't know. They call me the Golden Star. If they only knew how little gold there is in me. You know when

[ 117 ]

we came back last night my head was all in a whirl. And then my father and some of his men took me into the council hall and told me what they meant when they called me the Golden Star."

"Then tell me," he begged.

"I will tell you what I know. . . . It seems that in the past there has been much talk in the eastern lands of the coming of some great ruler who will bring peace. And in some way, years and years ago the coming of that ruler was likened to the appearance of a new star in the Heavens, and legend gave it the name of the Golden Star."

"Yes."

"And every nation and race hereabouts believed in that story, that there would some day come a leader and the leader's sign would be a star of gold."

"The Tartars as well as the Slavs?"

"Yes. . . . And the Greeks as well. Had King Kazimir resided in the eastern provinces as much as he has in the West, he certainly would have heard the story. Every minstrel and traveling Tsigan knows about it, my father said. . . . And when I was born in Suzdal where my father had taken my mother after the boyars had tried to kill him in a border city, there was present an astrologer—by chance, I think."

"Do you know his name?"

"No. A Greek though. . . . And on the night when I was born a star appeared in the Heavens which men had never seen before. And to this star the astrologer gave the name Golden Star. It might have been a comet, who can tell? But the fame of it spread like magic all over the East, and as a result I was known as the child of the Golden Star, though no one called me that to my face. But when the news went abroad, strange men began to come to our home in Suzdal to see me, and they brought many presents, and once an attempt was made to carry me off. Those who tried were Tartars, for they believed that I carried a charm and that if they possessed me and I became their ruler, they would win all their battles and would conquer the world."

"Then that is the reason," exclaimed Michael, "that the Poloviets tried to carry you off yesterday?"

"I am sure it is. But let me go on. . . . My mother died when I was very small, and my father, fearing lest there should be more attempts to obtain me, had me taken secretly to Chelm and put in a convent there. It was from there that I came to Halich."

"When did your father come here?"

"That I do not know. . . . But it was three years ago, he said, that his lord, Duke Dimitri of Suzdal, went to the city of Vladimir and proclaimed himself grand duke of all the Russias. For the grand duke, you know, is tsar. My father went with him, and there came also emissaries from other lands, the Tartars, the Greeks, and many others, but in order to actually establish himself as the ruler of all the Russias it was necessary that Dimitri go to Sarai, the capital of the Tartar empire, and there receive confirmation from the Khan of the Tartars, who is Murut."

"And did he go?"

"He is there now, but, Michael, another has also gone to Murut and demands that *he* be appointed grand duke of all the Russias. This other is also known as Dimitri, Dimitri of Moskva, and he is only twelve years old, but they say that the Holy Alexis of the Church in Moskva has chosen him. And all have gone to Murut, the Khan of the Tartars, and he will choose who the next grand duke is to be. And if he chooses Dimitri of Suzdal, the friend of my father, then my father will have as his ally in his plans the most powerful ruler in the Slav lands."

"Then it is the plan of your father to rule here, while Dimitri of Suzdal rules in the eastern Slav lands?"

"That is so."

"And in this way your father will be Duke of Halich, and he will have the support not only of Dimitri of Suzdal, but also of the Tartars, and the Lithuanians, and all these others that are here?"

"Yes," she said.

"Then," he puzzled a bit, "you as the Duke's daughter, the Golden Star men have prophesied about, will be the next ruler after the Duke? You are now here in Halich to bring good fortune to all these plans?"

"No." She turned to him excitedly. "Michael, that is not all of it. I am to be the ruler of an empire in which Dimitri and my father and the Tartars are rulers *under* me, and there is more to this than anyone can understand."

He only stared in astonishment. "For this is the prophecy which concerns the Golden Star," she went on. "The Golden Star is to rule, and only under her will come prosperity and peace. And according to the legend, her empire will be greater than any empire ever known to man, and it will extend from the Tartar land clear to the empire in Europe."

"But these others, these Greeks?"

"That is an important part of it all," she said. "There will be a new ruler in Tsargrad, and his empire will be part of ours, and we shall drive back the Turks from his realm."

Michael again was speechless. Then suddenly he broke out: "Then that empire which men call Byzantine is to be part of this empire. There is not much left of it now."

"Michael, it was in that land that the whole plan actually began. There is a monk in Thrace whom men call Joasaph, but he has not always been a monk. Men say that he is a deposed emperor."

"Well?"

"It is he who first sent messages to my father and Dimitri in

Suzdal.  He had heard of the legend of the Golden Star and, wishing to win back his empire which was called the Eastern Roman Empire, evolved this plan.  It is he who has furnished much of the money for rebuilding the ducal grod of Halich, for there is a party in Tsargrad ready to rise up and proclaim him ruler; it is he and this party who have sent the Greek fleet that now lies at anchor below the city."

"Have you seen him?"

"No.  He is not here in the city, I think, though he will be here when I am crowned."

"When will that be?"

"Tomorrow night perhaps."  She trembled as she said this and moved nearer toward him.  "Do you think that your people in Lvov would take care of me if I escaped to them?"

"They would—they would," he exclaimed.

"I fear for it all," she went on.  "I do not know how men accomplish things, but all this seems somehow so wild, so useless. There are so many people, so many purposes—and yet my father believes in it and says that it cannot go wrong.  But I am afraid, Michael.  I dare not leave the castle lest some one carry me away; the Tartars are not to be trusted, and you know what happened yesterday.  What will become of me if anything happens to my father?  These others here are selfish and only looking out for themselves. . . .  What is to become of me, I wonder?  Shall I remain here or shall I go to Tsargrad or shall I reign in Suzdal? There will be war with Poland perhaps, and with Hungary and with the Empire.  Michael . . . though it would break my father's heart, I hope that something will happen to spoil all these plans."

The boy's head whirled.  The immensity of it took away his power of reasoning for the moment, but he grasped at the nearest idea.  "It is all intrigue—I cannot see clearly, but you must tell your father of the dwarf·and the words of the astrologer in the crypt."

"It will do no good." For a long time she looked hopelessly at the view below. "Why are we so young?" she asked at length. "Men would only laugh at us if we spoke our minds, and yet I see in all this nothing but trouble. . . . My father has one dream, the re-establishment of the power of his fathers. . . . The Tartars seek a coalition which will give them more power. . . . The Lithuanians want land and peace, and the men of Suzdal want all the Russias. Then this emperor from the south wants his empire back again—and all of them are bound together by only one thing."

"And that?"

"The Golden Star. A legend, a story, a myth. And yet it is pretext enough for men to build empires on."

"Yet, all rulers trust the stars more than they trust anything else. No king goes out to battle before his astrologer reads the skies and selects the most favorable moment."

"I know it," she said, though her thoughts were still upon her own words.

Some women attendants came hurrying out of the palace and made inquiries of the guards; a man who had seen the children enter the tower pointed up toward the high wall where they sat, and at once Katerina heard someone calling her name. "They are hunting us. I must go down," she said.

They made their way back to the flooring and began to descend the tower stairs.

"I will say good-by until tomorrow night;" she turned about to him as he stood above her. "You know it is the custom of the people of the East that women shall keep their faces hidden. My father does not agree, but others who are here will think that we are not in sympathy with them if we do not observe their customs. And so from this time until the coronation you will not see my face. Indeed, it will be better if I am not seen talking with you, so I will go ahead."

He hesitated until she disappeared, then followed slowly until he reached the court; by that time she had gone in with the servants. His thoughts were revolving rapidly, now touching upon this, now upon that; what would happen when Stasko told his father about the gathering at Halich? What would happen to Katerina if she were actually crowned empress of an empire that did not exist? What would be his own fate if the Duke were removed from power by the intrigues of these others? And then he began to wonder at the strangeness of it all! But as he wondered it did not seem so strange after all and a glimmering of the truth came to him; here were vigorous minds putting into execution a plot that, although well-nigh desperate, still bore some evidences of reasonable success. A grand duke in Suzdal or Vladimir, another in Halich, a khan in Sarai, an emperor in Tsargrad, and all of them subject to a fantastic ruler whose destiny had been written in the stars.

And as well as a boy might comprehend a huge plot that included a half-dozen races and kingdoms he understood something of that which had passed before his eyes. For the men of Christendom were planning to raise a Third Rome upon earth, the first Rome having passed away, and the second which men called Byzantium, or Constantinople, or Tsargrad being now in danger of extinction from the Turks. And to raise a Third Rome, the arms of Christians were not sufficient; there were necessary the arms of Mohammedans and Pagans. Therefore one could not make a coalition beneath some Christian Emperor; it was necessary to have a ruler whom the pagan could obey as well. And for that, it had been noised about among those who were not Christians that a great prophecy of the East had come to pass, that a Golden Star had arisen, and would unite all men, Christians and those of other creeds as well. This Golden Star was the daughter of Duke Lev. And he who had conceived this whole tangled plot was a monk in Thrace.

The picture of the fire tubes came into his mind.

"I will go back and look at them," he thought.

But as he glanced up, for his eyes had been upon the stones of the court while he had pondered, he saw that he had wandered across to the second of the twin towers which guarded the Cathedral gate. As the door to this also lay open he went in quickly and was soon mounting the stairs.

# CHAPTER IX

## THE SINKING OF THE GALLEY

BY what mischance in climbing the stairs he did not hear voices above him, it would be impossible to speculate upon. Perhaps his thoughts were busy running over the details of the information given to him by Katerina—perhaps the spell of her presence was upon him still, with the blood surging in his cheeks and his heart beating joyously. Alas that he did not hear these voices! For a running conversation had been going on at least fifteen minutes before he emerged through the opening at the top of the stairs, a conversation between Phokas, the astrologer, and the dwarf who answered to the name Krok. And had he heard this conversation it would have led him to follow his half-formed determination, to go to Duke Lev and acquaint him with the whole story of his adventures in the crypt.

Instead he stumbled directly upon them.

Phokas was standing close to the wall opposite the place where the stairs emerged. The dwarf was at his feet, squatting like a toad, as it seemed to Michael in that first shuddering surprise, when the realization of what he had come upon struck him with the force of a smart blow.

"The boy himself!" exclaimed the astrologer.

Michael drew back, but the dwarf had leaped like a flash to block his escape. Backing to the wall and fervently berating himself for being about without even a knife, the boy closed his fists and waited for the attack.

It came, but not as he had suspected. Phokas was closing in to break down his guard when, with the agility of a serpent, the dwarf entangled the boy's legs, snapped them out from under him, and sent him hurtling against the wall. Michael opened his lips to shout, hoping that someone in the court below would hear his voice. He had been too proud to shout before; now, it was too late. First the dwarf's hand, and then the astrologer's white cap went across his mouth. Phokas secured the gag, while Krok sat on his chest.

Suddenly the former laughed. "What fortune we had here!"

"Yes. He will carry no tales," answered the dwarf. "Has he spoken already?"

"No. He had no chance last night, and today the Duke is out with his boyars."

"He may have told the girl."

"We must chance that."

They spoke in the old dialect of the Halich lands, the dialect of Rus.

"Shall I cut his windpipe?" asked Krok, taking a knife from his belt.

"No. I do not dare. It is too great a risk. We must get him away from here."

"How to do that?" asked the other putting his knife back, regretfully.

"Take him to the crypt. I will give you a hand. At nightfall we can remove him to the galleys. No one will search for him there."

The dwarf nodded. Phokas went on: "When he does not appear today they will think that he has escaped. He is a spy here in any case and would be likely to try another escape. We will take him to the ships."

"Which one?"

# THE SINKING OF THE GALLEY

"The one that goes down the river tonight. The galley that takes the messages to our friends in Tsargrad. By tomorrow he will be far from here."

Half-stunned from the blow which he had received in his fall, Michael but little realized what all the conversation meant. He knew, after one long terrible moment when the dwarf held his knife in his hands, that they would not kill him. The word galleys, however, he recognized, and it brought a sinking of heart, for men all over the Slav lands knew what the word galleys implied. For on them were chained in long rows the slaves who had been taken prisoners in war; their duty was to row the galley through the water, and they were held in their seats by heavy chains, scourged, starved, worked to exhaustion, and usually drowned when the galley was overcome by an enemy and sunk. But the hideousness of all this was not so keen in his thoughts because of the blow which had blunted his senses, and as they carried him stealthily down the tower stairs and swung him cautiously about the tower into the passage leading into the crypt, his wits wandered and he imagined himself at home and thought that the men who were carrying him were boys playing a trick upon him.

In the crypt the coolness of the air revived him presently, and brought back the realization of his fate. The cloth was still upon his jaws; he was lying on the flat top of a tomb, with the dwarf squatting on guard just below him. His feet and arms were securely fastened. In his eyes played the flickering red light which danced up and down and sideways before the shrine; the picture which it lighted seemed like a scene from a dream— and indeed life itself seemed a dream, a thing of shadows that shifted constantly in a dancing light.

The astrologer was not there. His head ached terribly. Once the dwarf forced some bread between his teeth and poured a kind of Hungarian wine down his throat. Then he slept, but dreams of a distorted fancy tormented him, and he kept coming back to the point of consciousness only to sink to sleep again. Bells sounded somewhere. Another time he heard someone opening a door far away in the darkness. Would it not be possible to escape? In his delirium he fancied that he might roll over upon the dwarf and reach the knife in his belt and cut the ropes that bound him. Then he could escape by the vaulted way into his own room.

Then for no reason at all he abandoned his thoughts of escape and began to wonder about Katerina. Katerina was the Golden Star of Halich. That was what the King wanted to know. If he could only return to tell him! But then, Stasko would find his father and his father would report to the King . . . Poor Katerina. What would her lot be? Would her father be able to protect her in the midst of all these people who wanted her? Would they take her to Tsargrad? If the plan failed what would become of her then? Who would have thought on that first day in the Tsigan camp that she was the Golden Star, and that it was for her coming that the city of Halich was being restored to its former glory?

Suddenly he felt the dwarf's hands upon him. He would have cried out, had not shame prevented him, for the grip was like that of pincers. He was shifted from the tomb, raised upon the creature's back and carried along through the crypt rapidly. Before the point where the stairs went up to the Cathedral, the dwarf turned to the right through a passage unknown to Michael; this he traversed rapidly with the step of one well used to its twistings, and in a few minutes they were in the open air. It was late at night, Michael discovered—the moon had set and the stars glistened overhead like white fires.

In an endeavor to mark the locality, Michael turned his head and saw the castle and the Cathedral rising against the dark sky over behind them; they were on the east slope of Krylos Hill, beyond the wall. And now there were other figures about, and horses. He was passed up to a man on horseback, who did not grip him as the dwarf had done. A word was given, they were off, riding down a slope and over a little bridge, then up another slope and off to the left along a well-beaten road. After some distance of such traveling a second horseman who had been accompanying them turned and went back, leaving the man who carried Michael to ride on alone. At the distance of a long arrow's flight from this place he turned off to the east again, following a narrow path across a line of hills, in the direction of what was later known as Pitrycz, but turning to the south before reaching Pitrycz, he came to the water's edge near the collection of peasants' houses which took the name Kozina. Here, Michael could hear the Dniester river flowing over its pebbly bed.

For some curious reason hope returned to him with the sound of the flowing water. It was as if the river were friendly, even though men were not friendly. They followed the bank in a southerly direction for a while, until a small light seemed to leap at them from the darkness, and they stopped by the side of a Grecian galley that lay close to shore, with a lantern of some kind high up in the stern. The horseman shouted, there came the noise of men running on the galley's deck. A plank was shoved out and the horseman leaped from the saddle with Michael in his arms and went aboard the galley.

There was no conversation. The galley was a small one, with a single mast, a space for perhaps twelve rowers, a dragon on the prow, and a long spike extending from the high deck aft in the manner of a ram. Michael at once perceived that matters had been well arranged; two men took him silently from the horseman, loosened the ropes from his feet and hands, and tore the gag

[ 129 ]

from his mouth. Then they led him down an incline to a small open space on the deck, and thrust him through an opening into a little forecastle just under the dragon on the prow. There was barely room enough to lie there upon a pile of ropes; the entrance behind him was barred by heavy wooden crates.

He thanked his own luck that he was not taken to the rowers' bench at once. Evidently different orders had been sent. From the deck he had had one glance at the rowers—they were all swarthy Ethiopians—sleeping with their heads upon their arms.

Preparations were going forward busily on the deck. Other horsemen came riding up beside the ship, and cargo was brought aboard. There was the sound of coiling ropes, of clanking chains —the rowers were being awakened; they sighed loudly as they yawned. "God spare me from that fate," he prayed.

The galley carried a sail, but in a river sails were treacherous, and besides there were rapids and one could not veer from the current.

More freight was brought aboard. Heavy footsteps sounded close above his head as if someone in authority were making a last inspection. Orders were given sharply though in a low tone; the landing plank came in, oars were going down—they were pushing off. And before it came upon him to scream at the top of his voice, the men on shore had pushed the boat out on to the water, the steersman was at the stern, and the oars were catching at the black water. It swung out into the current, trembled, and then darted ahead.

"I will sleep through this," Michael thought. "My mind will be stronger if I sleep, and I may have a chance to escape. If they go clear to Tsargrad it will take many days, and it may be there might come Polish scouting parties along the bank . . . I wonder what they are taking me to? But I will sleep and hope." He clung to hope desperately, but he could not sleep. His head still ached a little where the dwarf had stunned him against the wall, and his brain pounded with the throb of excitement and apprehension.

And even now there were no words spoken upon the galley. The crew worked silently, shifting the cargo and trimming the vessel as for a long voyage. In their places the rowers swayed back and forth—he could hear them as the benches creaked beneath them, and with each play of oars the vessel shot rapidly ahead with the current. Far away in the woods above the banks could be heard now the hooting of an owl, now the baying of some wild animal. The river murmured as the sharp prow cut its waters, and all at once the rowers began to sing a little song, in low tones, keeping tune and accenting the rhythm with sweep of the oar and beating of the foot. Who were these men, he wondered; captives, prisoners, slaves and yet singing! The song was of the East, and their voices were deep and mysterious as is the East, and the spell of the East lay over them all.

On and on they went; faster and faster moved the oars; faster and faster rose the cadence of their song. . . .

Then all at once out of the silence of the night there went up a most hideous crash. It was followed by the shrill shrieking of men, the rending of timbers, the rush of waters as if a cataract were at hand. Michael felt the compartment in which he had been imprisoned torn across as if it were paper, a beam violently sagging hurled him forward into the darkness, and black water closed about him. For a moment he knew that death was not far away—paralyzed with a sudden fear he surrendered himself to the flood; then all at once, shot with a burst of hope, he struck out with arms and feet to swim with the current. And with the action came exultation; he was free! In the dark night there would be none to see or pursue, the bank lay not far away and once upon it he would find freedom.

# THE GOLDEN STAR OF HALICH

But what of the galley? It was lurching and plunging in mid-stream with the galley slaves shrieking for help and the crew giving orders. Now and then a splash announced that someone had leaped overboard to save himself by swimming. The galley was doomed then. He swam out of the course of the ship which, now half-submerged, was swinging helplessly like a bobbing cork, its prow below water, its stern perilously low. And as he drove himself forward to escape the whirl that was forming about it, it suddenly plunged to the bottom of the river carrying with it the cargo and the rowers, whose shouts for help died out in a terrible silence. A bit of the current picked the boy up and swung him around, a wave from the sinking craft dragged him back; a whirlpool clawed at him with tenacious fingers, but he fought it off and struck out for open water. All that he wished to do now was to escape from the crew of the ship; they would look for him immediately they reached the shore, he knew that, and if it came now to a struggle with them or a struggle with fiercest rapids he would choose the rapids. The bubbling current lifted him ahead suddenly—he was in it, and away from the sunken ship— he had escaped. A shout of triumph was on his lips and he thrust out his arms in the darkness—when suddenly a pair of strong arms reached down and grasped him, and he was lifted clear out of the water and laid upon a surface that was secure.

He fought bitterly, but the arms held on. And the reaction from the shock and the plunge into cold water suddenly left him bereft of strength. He gave in, hopelessly, in despair; he could not see where he was, nor who had pulled him from the water, but he thought for the moment that it was some one of the enemy in another galley or a small boat. The thought of his desperate plight brought some blood back to his heart; the water was not far away, he would roll back. They could not stop him. And then, like the sound of an angel's voice from Heaven he heard in pure Polish above him : "It is the boy, the friend of Stasko. . . . How did you come here ?"

"Tsigani," he murmured and the joy sent his heart leaping. "Where am I ?"

"On the raft. The galley ran into it." And then he realized what had happened. For the galley, sweeping downstream, had taken no account of the obstacles that lay in its path. Or if a man had been on lookout, the raft was so low that he must have failed to see it. And in such a case, woe to the vessel which collided with the Tsigan raft, for the raft was built of the thickest logs of the forest, fastened together by the toughest thongs and able to ride even the rapids at Yampol. Against this raft, the galley had dashed while being propelled at full speed by its rowers; no ship of that day could have withstood such a shock. Michael was on his feet in an instant.

"The men in the galley; are they lost?"

Across the dark water there was no sound of life. The stars shone down upon its blackness, and the Tsigan eyes which see like cats could make out no moving shapes nor any swimming men. Those few who had thrown themselves into the water were by this time upon the bank and probably running back with news of the disaster, but the greater number, surprised and stunned by the shock of the collision, had gone down with the ship. And when Michael realized this, he fell upon his knees and thanked God for his delivery.

There was no inactivity upon the raft however. Men and women were rushing hither and thither with long poles, stemming the raft's progress and thrusting out planks in the hopes that some person from the wreck might be struggling by. It was, as it proved, a useless task. The bulging hulk had sucked in most of those upon its deck, and all those who were below, with the exception of Michael. The unfortunate rowers had found deliverance from their captivity at last.

And dimly in the starlight might be seen rising to the surface pieces of wood, odds and ends that had cluttered the decks, a broken oar, some old clothing, a section of a mast with the pennant still upon it, a bit of tackle. The Tsigani had poled their raft back close to the spot where the galley had gone down, but there was no shape nor sound nor shadow of a craft there now.

"They are lost," exclaimed the Tsigan leader. "Draw in your poles."

They floated around again, and the current caught them. "We will land you," he said to Michael. "From the farther bank you can make your way to Bolshov and join the Poles there. It will be no task to pole you across, and then we must be on our way to Kamenets. Should they find us here now, they might think that we were to blame in this matter." He pointed upstream.

For the first time since his capture in the tower Michael drew a breath free from anxiety. Here he was now in the hands of friends, the friendly bank not far away, his father at Bolshov just beyond; it would be easy to make one's way warily through the forest or even follow the stream until he came to the flats. His own danger in the matter was at an end. "Not fifteen minutes ago I was a prisoner bound for Tsargrad," he thought; "now I am free and will soon be in my father's camp."

The Tsigan touched his arm. "Inside that house you will find a fire." Michael stared into the darkness and saw much to his surprise that the "house" was a small cabin built of logs near the front of the raft; all rafts carried such structures for shelter for the women and also for protection of food during rainstorms. The boy hurried forward and found a fire blazing upon a metal brazier; he took off his clothes and wrung out the water and held them close to the flame. It was a poor method, for the cloth was singed in many places, but it did the business quite quickly.

In the meantime the raft was being driven across the stream diagonally to a place where a landing could be made. The Tsigan held the raft there until Michael's steaming garments became dryer and then exclaimed, "We must go."

But Michael turned upon him, clad only to the waist, holding his cape up to the blaze: "I have decided not to go."

"What?"

"No. You can put me down on the other bank. I will go back to Krylos." The determination had flashed through his brain while he stood there drying his clothes. "My father has received from Stasko all the information he needs. I should be of little use that way."

"But your enemies are on that side."

"I know. But there is someone there I would help. A friend."

The Tsigan said nothing but cast off the raft again, and in a few minutes they were back on the Halich side. "So . . . " he said, "it will be as you wish."

Michael drew on his cape; it was still damp though it would soon dry upon his body. Then with a word of thanks to the Tsigan he ran to the edge of the raft and leaped ashore. The footing was good; indeed a hard sand extended out into the river. Beyond the beach was a forest and through it several trails to Krylos. The next instant the raft was poled out again, and the voices from it lingered in his ears a moment; he turned his back upon them and followed the sand until he came to a place where the trail ran near to the river. Here he swung to the left and disappeared among the trees.

# CHAPTER X

## MICHAEL BECOMES A MAN

THE ducal grod, Krylos, lying in the midst of the old city of Halich occupies a geographical position that makes it easy of approach from all sides. This may have been due to the course of the Dniester river which inclosed the old city on two sides and partly on the third. It left the land on which the settlement had been, a peninsula almost; therefore when Michael struck out through the woods he had only to go directly west in order to reach the main roads running the length of the peninsula. He had figured out his direction and his distances in very short time, for when one put his back to the river he was facing the west, with the north upstream and the south down. The galley had brought him a quarter of a mile perhaps below the place where the horseman had carried him on board, and there was some distance gained in addition because of the double crossing of the Tsigan raft. If he kept moving to the west he was bound to come out on the road which ran by Krylos—the old road of the Romans—and the road which led to Wallachia.

As he went through the woods, looking up overhead to the stars that shone between the branches, he seemed for the time being to be a part of a new and marvelous world. He had never been through these woods before, but he was confident of the path, and he felt no fear. Indeed the contrast between these sheltering trees and the hatred of Phokas and the dwarf was enough to

# MICHAEL BECOMES A MAN

lighten any heart; and in addition to that he was swept by a great emotion that lifted him up from little fears.

Hitherto in his life he had been concerned only with his own affairs. His thoughts from infancy had been upon matters relating to himself. It had seemed as if his mother and father lived only to serve his needs; he was not so selfish as that all the time, though there were moments when he truly felt as if the whole world were designed merely for his own pleasure, his own benefit. It is not a rare feeling either, in the years of youth when all life is inviting, and romance and adventure everywhere beckon.

But something had come over him. It had all the earmarks of a miracle. For the first time in his life he was deliberately putting aside his own wishes and desires, indeed his own security and safety, in order to help someone else. In that moment of brilliant vision on the raft when it had been his intent to step ashore and hasten to Bolshov to join his father, there had come into his mind the picture of this girl, this friend, alone in the midst of unknown perils. She had been his comrade—they had sworn to help each other; the running away from danger came over him as that which only a coward would do. And with that decision to go back, something else had happened; the feeling of self that he had always known changed somewhat. It was more important now that he put self aside, and in so doing he had entered into another world.

How bright was the light of the stars! How much alive were the trees; how responsive was every breath of wind; and these things were all his own. It even seemed as if something far away were singing, a choir perhaps, perhaps his own heart, and with it happiness descended upon him. The music changed and became the melody of a great orchestra—to its cadence were woven old familiar tunes, new tunes also surging through him as he went along the path. It was a new world.

# THE GOLDEN STAR OF HALICH

He realized, too, that this new world was forever opened to him, that the old days of concern over nothing but self had gone forever. Katerina, his friend, belonged in the new world. In a sense it was a world which they two alone knew, a world of adventure and romance, and to achieve such a world there had been necessary self-renunciation on his own part. He felt the truth and the reality of that which had seemed at first a vision, and out of the pulsation of his senses came the pictures of a life of glory and realization.

His life as he had lived it seemed at once far away and undesirable, even a trifle mean; the new world was the world of other people, of other things, the world of great adventure. And there came to him an appreciation of the beauty of men's lives, and the deeds which they did, and the triumphs they accomplished. . . . He had chosen to risk his life to help another person. There was not much he could do, and yet he must do this thing, he could not desert such a friend. He would go back and wait with her; perhaps delivery for them all was not far away; perhaps his father with the Polish knights was even then riding to the rescue.

The night waned, and the morning star arose. And as it shone brilliantly before the sun came to dim it, he turned toward it with rapture in his heart, music in his ears. "You are my star," he exclaimed. "You are my Golden Star of Halich."

# CHAPTER XI

## THE SINGER FROM THE STEPPE

AS he went on the forest seemed to open before him. The pine needles were soft beneath his steps; his swelling heart found such communion with the sky and the air that he felt himself almost to be floating, and all the time the sound of majestic music roared in his ears. He knew that he must bend his course to the north so that he might come to the entrance where the road struck directly to the west and to the castle on Krylos; in the course of several hours he reached the place where he should have turned, but he was treading so lightly upon earth, his head was so immersed in the skies, that he did not notice the turning and followed another path, this one leading directly south toward the place where the new town of Halich flanked itself about the steep hill where a new fortification was rising.

He knew that he had not gone a great distance in the galley—though practical things for the nonce were out of his head; still he had followed instinctively a route that he thought would bring him back to Krylos. And when practical thoughts did come at last, without realizing that he had strayed from his course, he did realize that it would be dangerous to meet any person other than the Duke's own bodyguard; he must make himself known to that guard and be taken before the Duke. For should he meet any of the other troops, or the men of the astrologer Phokas, the chances were that he would be seized again and put upon another galley and without any such chances of escape a second time. As he now and then threw his mind upon the occurrences of the night before, he could not help realizing how like a miracle the whole thing had been. To avoid further danger he must keep aloof from all strangers and armed men. Perhaps he would need to hide in the woods near the castle until one of the Duke's men came out, or he saw an opportunity to slip inside the gate. There was caution to be observed at all times and in all places.

It began to grow light. The birds had commenced their melody with the first streak of gray in the sky; the river was still at his right, he noted, as the dawn came upon the world and a bit of cold silver glittered off in the distance. To the left the woods were still thick, and ahead ran a well-trodden path; he followed it, wondering at just what point he would be obliged to turn and cross the ridge by which he had been led to the galley. He did not realize yet that he had long since passed it, but he did realize suddenly that something was wrong when he noticed that there was a clearing in the trees ahead and that the tops of thatched houses were appearing.

"I saw no houses when I came," he thought. Then he began to wonder if he had taken the wrong road. "No—there is the river to my right. Krylos must lie to my left through the trees. But these houses! Surely the peasants would not build in a clearing in the wood. This must be part of a village." He went ahead, on the alert now, his high spirits for the moment in abeyance; cautiously he approached the trees at the edge of the wood and looked out.

"Yes, it's like the edge of a village. Where can I be?" One house lay directly in front, to the left four or five others in a cluster. Across a well-beaten road which turned just beyond these and, sweeping to the left up a hill, disappeared, stood two very old houses in decay; of them there was left little save stone foundations.

And then it came to him. He had passed the turning where the side road ran off to Krylos. He had gone on beyond until he now stood at the edge of the new town. There was nothing to do but to put back into the woods. He turned to go back.

But this time he saw a sight that froze him into a statue momentarily. The woods behind him were full of men. They were coming along the path he had just traveled, they were coming in from the right and from the left—soldiers, strange men clad in skins of animals but with round breast-plates, pointed helmets, and long axes upon their shoulders. "Lithuanians," he thought— then, "Rus"—but there was no time to speculate. Luckily he had passed beyond a high hedge at the wood border and for the moment he was not seen, though he knew that it would not be possible to escape detection for long. Behind him the woods were full both toward the right and toward the left, as if an army had entered the forest—it was fortunate that they had not seen him before. Perhaps they had been coming up from the river bank and were passing in open order through the forest.

"That must be it," he reasoned. "Could I but reach those ruined house walls beyond the peasant cottages I might escape."

He lowered himself to the ground, ran a few steps on all-fours, then skirting about the first peasant cottage put it between himself and the men in the woods. A dog began to bark—the soldiers began to shout at each other. "I wonder if they have seen me," he thought, and disregarding all caution, fled like the wind for the highway and the ruined house in its elbow.

The soldiers had noticed something, for a number of them came hurrying out of the woods and started to run toward the first peasant cottage, where a dog was now barking fiercely. "They are hunting someone—perhaps me," thought Michael. "I must make that wall."

He reached it, hesitated one moment as he realized that if he had been seen he was but entering a trap—then, knowing that it was his one hope of safety, threw all his energy into one terrific leap, over the crumbling brick wall.   The desperate impulse took him high enough—he flew for a moment it seemed between Heaven and earth, and then alighted with a thud.   But it was a living thud that came from beneath him.   He had not landed on hard ground or floor or stones as he had expected; he had landed on something soft, something that groaned and made an exclamation that was short, pointed, and wrathful.   His feet luckily had straddled the creature who lay there supine—it was his body that came in contact with huge ribs and a high stomach.   Like a flash the man upon whom he had alighted had arisen to his knees and, turning over quickly like some animal, hostile and upon all-fours, glared at the boy.

He did not glare long.   "Help me," said Michael desperately, beneath his breath, for the eyes and face that looked at him were kind; "help me, for enemies are pursuing me."   In his excitement he had spoken in pure Polish.

And it was in pure Polish that the reply came: "Willingly I will, but why jump upon my chest?   I am an old man; I earn my living by playing and singing from town to town; why tempt fortune by risking my curse?"

"Listen."   The boy crouched down.   Outside the wall the soldiers were hurrying along, and talking in a language that he could not understand.

"Ha, Lithuanian," exclaimed the other, looking at the boy curiously.   "Yes.   I will save you.   They have not seen you.   And what do you do here?"

"Sh,"—Michael paled.   His heart was pounding like water over a rock.   The men might hear and then where would he be?

The soldiers went on toward the town.   He took a long breath

[ 142 ]

at that and looked at the man he had alighted on. He was an old man just as he had said; he had white hair that fell about his shoulders. His beard, long and white, fell almost to his waist. Huge in stature, he wore a long gray robe that was caught with a piece of rope that served for a girdle. And in the farther hand, clutched as if for safety, was a queer-looking thing—a piece of wood, with strings, and a small crank at the end. What had he said? He earned his living by playing and singing. The significance of it flashed upon Michael. This was a minstrel, a minstrel of the border, perhaps a Polish minstrel, for he spoke Polish so well.

"They have gone," the man exclaimed, "they have not seen you."

Michael suddenly started. The wet nose of a dog had touched his hand. Looking down he saw a small dirty animal, flea-bitten, unbeautiful, with short white and black hair—gazing up at him with keen eyes and wagging zealously his stump of a tail.

"Down, Fox," said the old man.

The dog went close to the wall and snuggled down there, after turning about once or twice.

"A good dog," exclaimed the old man.

Michael was nervous lest he should bark. "That he will not," exclaimed the other as if reading his thoughts. The boy saw that he had merry blue eyes.

"Hush, they are coming back." Hugging the wall closely he moved not a hair until the soldiers were back in the woods again.

"I do not think they saw me."

"No. Who are you?" The old man brushed himself and looked into the boy's eyes. "I like you, though you did nearly kill me with surprise."

"Of the Korzets."

"You bear the Korzets' crest? Of Lvov?"

"Yes."

"Then God be with you. I know your family well. It must have been your father who in the old days often gave me his fire to sleep by. True Lechs they are."

"Poles."

"I know. But I love the old name. Here on the steppe we think of our fatherland as the land of the Lechs, and God knows why they traded off a good name for a strange one. But how come you here?"

The boy, feeling the keen sympathy of the old man, unbosomed himself at once. It was a long story, and he told it in a low voice, fearing lest the soldiers should return. And as he told it the old man kept nodding his head and exclaiming, "As I thought," until he reached the very end. At the end he leaped into the air, and then Michael saw the immensity of his bulk; turning to the boy he said in a tense voice:

"It is for all this that I am here."

"You?"

"Yes. For when there comes the report of things like this it is for us to be here to note what happens. As we travel up and down the land, in the city, or on the steppe, folk ask us always what there is of note. I am a minstrel—that is my calling. Nature always draws the wolf to the forest. Were I a warrior then it would be my work to be here as well. But I must see all that happens here, and then I shall record it in my mind. I shall make a tale of it and a song, and then in years to come he whom I have taught will sing the song of all that happens here, to future generations. And he will teach another, and that one will teach another, and so all this will not be lost, but men may know what things were great in our day."

"What is your name?"

"Men call me the Wanderer."

"Have you no other name?"

"None that I know.   But is not that enough?"

Michael thought very hard.   "But what of your Christian name?   How will Christ know you when you come to Paradise?"

The old man smiled and in his smile was music and perchance Paradise itself.

"The good Christ need know no such man as I.   But when I come to the gates of Paradise then will I say, 'Has any angel's harp need of stringing?'   I will sit me down by the gate and I will tune the harps and I will fit new strings, for over all the steppes from Sarai to Halich, over the land of the Lechs from Lvov to Krakow there is no such one as I to string harps and make the strings mindful of their proper music.   For work and a good heart, God will repay."

Michael was satisfied.   "I must go back to the castle," he said after a while, stroking the dog's head as he spoke.

"How will you go?"

"Through the woods."

The old man shook his head."That you may not.   They are full of soldiers and will be all day."

"Then how may I go?"

The Wanderer hummed between his teeth, which were white and strong despite his years.

"You must go with me by the high road."

"With you?"

"Yes."   The old man took up the object which lay by his side, and fondled its strings.   "This is my organistrum," he said.   "I am a minstrel who has the right to wander like a Tsigan wherever he lists—in the domains of duke, king, or Tsar.   I play in the courts, in the roads, in the cities, and wherever I wish.   You shall go with me; I like you and you are a Lech and I am a Lech. Here—" he pulled loose a part of his cape and threw it over the boy's shoulder; "turn your cap inside out and lead my dog upon his string. I shall be the minstrel and you will be the minstrel's boy."

Michael adjusted the cape about him. It fell clear to his ankles, covering his water-stained clothes; the cap was twisted about in a twinkling, and there he stood the very picture of a minstrel's boy.

"We shall see great things, you and I," said the old man. "I knew far off there in the steppe that the world was about to come to an end."

Michael stared. The Wanderer was looking out into space, over his head, as if he saw him not at all.

"There is confusion over all the lands, the Rus are on the march —the two Dimitris are gone to Murut, the Tartar, and each asks to be crowned with the crown of the grand duke. There is Dimitri of Suzdal and Dimitri of Moskva, whom the holy Alexis leads. Whoever wins—then there will be war. Olgerd the Lithuanian is upon the march—his men are here now. Tartars are moving from east to west. King Kazimir too is on the march—"

Michael burst in, "Do you know that? Did the Tsigan reach him?"

But the Wanderer paid no attention to him. "There are others too, Bulgarians, Czechs, Hungarians—the tribes of the Polovtsy as well—but there is one greater than all these. He is a monk. He has been an emperor—he comes here"—the minstrel seemed to be in a trance. And yet to Michael it was not strange, for men like this, wanderers, were believed to possess the power to read the future—they were considered holy by all the people, and they were known to have certain occult powers.

"He comes here," went on the Wanderer, "to find the Golden Star. And I come here as well to find the Golden Star. Long has it been read in the stars that out of the House of the Lion will come the Golden Star, and when the Golden Star rises over the East then will the miracle be performed." His eyelids, all tense the moment before, began to tremble, the spell left them—"We must sleep first," he exclaimed turning to the boy as if he were merely continuing a conversation. "Lie down by the wall and sleep. The sun will not strike us here, and later we will go out and perhaps earn a meal, and then go to the castle."

Michael drew the cape about him and rolled close to the wall. He was sleepy—sleep had been driven from his eyes by sheer excitement up to this very moment; but something in the manner of the man brought the realization upon him like a blow—how sleepy he was! He yawned, and with the yawn sank into a deep, untroubled sleep.

He was awakened by the dog lapping at his hand, sent by command of the minstrel who stood at a little distance girding up his long robe and tightening his belt. As he rose the dog darted back to his master and, at a raised finger, crouched before him, looking up into his eyes with adoration and slapping the ground with the stumpy tail. Michael drew himself together, stood up a moment stupidly, then with returning animation pulled back the disguise over his clothes and exclaimed, "I'm ready."

"Whoever rises early, to him God gives, but we must first earn our dinner," said the Wanderer. "You see this?" He pointed to the musical instrument which lay on the ground near him; it was a curious, box-like affair as Michael saw now at close range, like the body of a violin without the fretted stick. There were strings running across it as on a violin, but sloping in close at the lower end there was a wheel. Connecting with this wheel was a short, round piece of metal which ran to a revolving lever on the outside of the box. By turning the lever with one hand and depressing the strings against the wheel, the musician could obtain any simple tune he wished, and indeed such skill did most of these traveling musicians possess that they could play chords and even shift from one part to another.

This instrument the Wanderer suspended from his left shoulder so that it hung beneath the arm where he could crook his elbow and hold it securely. In the other hand he took up a staff, crooked at the top like a shepherd's staff. "Come"—he whistled at the dog and beckoned at Michael, and they passed out of the ruined house together into the main road, boldly now, since in boldness was their safety to lie. The sun was just past the meridian, it was a warm day with a mist gathering from the river, and although Michael felt uncomfortable and stuffy beneath the cape he did not dare to unloose it.

They passed a few houses, bolted, and with shuttered doors; evidently the population was lying in wait for some event, or hiding from marauders. Now and then they would see signs of activity ahead as if a peasant was watering his horses on returning from a market, and again there would come sounds of chopping or the creaking of a wheel upon a well. But as they rounded the turn into the main part of the village it seemed as if they had come into the city of the dead, for there was not even a shadow stirring in the dusty, ill-kept roads.

"Is there no one here?" asked Michael.

"They are all here," answered the musician, "but they are all afraid."

"Do they fear the Tartars?"

"They fear the unknown. Strange doings are going on—strange armies lie about them. Too often have they seen their fields burned and their houses pillaged. They are lying close."

"Then how can we find anything to eat?"

"Man holds the bow, but God speeds the arrow. I will show you." The man walked along for a distance, past more closed huts, until he came to an opening nearly under the cliff where in times less eventful than these took place the exchanges of goods and the bargainings which went on daily in the village—the place of the fairs and the markets. Here in the very middle of this open space, about which were built the wretched-looking dwelling places of the town, he seated himself upon a stone and unloosed the musical instrument from his shoulder. "Wait until they hear this. . . . Then every mother's son of them will rush hither to learn the news and find out why I have come."

It flashed upon Michael that the musician spoke straight truth. In the early days, along the Eastern border, there were few couriers from town to town save these traveling minstrels. Indeed the minstrels were not only couriers but even journals with all the news of the day listed. Not of the day, perhaps, for the news they brought was often months old, but they were the only means that the poorer folk had of learning what the world was about. And there was something heroic about the way in which they recounted the news; great nobles were always careful never to ill-treat a minstrel, for the minstrel was often their means for handing down their exploits to posterity. Should a battle be fought it was the minstrel who recounted the feats of the heroes; something of an actor, the minstrel mimicked often the actions of the brave men, or perhaps like a jester made fun of the actions of cowards or stupid ones. Much license he had, too; he would act the part of a new-crowned king, he would strut like the newest-knighted lords. Then too if he came from the centers where King Kazimir had established courts of justice, he would tell who were in the courts and what privileges or penalties had been handed out to petitioners or prisoners.

So now, when the Wanderer sounded a few strains upon his organistrum, the peasants would undoubtedly come forth to learn what was in the air. They were probably ignorant as to what was going on here and knew only that their town was full of strange soldiers and enemies. The minstrel tightened his string, flipped the revolving lever about once or twice to be sure that it worked, then suddenly depressing the strings with his fingers, snapped off a gay air that leaped up into the air like rays of sunshine broken in water. As he played, Michael and the dog sat on the ground beside him, Michael with his right hand across the dog's neck.

Down fell the bars across the nearest peasant house. Out came a head that surveyed the market place up and down. Out stepped a peasant beckoning through the door and after him came a woman and a bevy of small children. Down went the bars from the next house, the next, and the next—out came the peasants tumbling like ants when a high hill is knocked over; boys and girls holding hands and racing in the sunshine, overjoyed to be freed. The town suddenly came to life; it was as if the heart had been dead and now started to beat. On came the people running and dancing and leaping, though not saying a word as yet for there was the expression of fear upon every face. They approached the market place, crossed it, and swept down upon the three, the Wanderer, Michael, and the dog. Trusting to their eyes that now all was well, since the minstrel had returned, or at least confident that they might learn what was in the air, they broke suddenly into a torrent of speaking; they whispered first, spoke louder, shouted, and the air was filled with the noise of voices just as solitude is broken when a traveler, passing through a peaceful valley, comes suddenly upon a waterfall. All the people spoke together—they questioned, they began to shout. Then suddenly the Wanderer put down his instrument and leaping to his feet pointed toward the farther corner of the market place over in the direction of the river; the boy got to his feet too, and the people turned quickly.

There approaching them was another old man, the very counterpart of the Wanderer. He too had long hair and flowing beard—he too wore a loose robe that fell to his ankles, caught in however with a costly belt of black silk. And under his right arm he carried a musical instrument, but his instrument was a small harp.

"Hail," shouted the Wanderer in Polish.

"I salute," rejoined the other in the tongue of the old Rus.

"What a miracle!" exclaimed everyone together. "What a miracle that two minstrels should be here at once! May the Blessed Lord and His Apostles bless this day that brings us two of them." And many of the people would have fallen before the venerable men and kissed the hems of their robes, only that the old men forbade them.

The newcomer swept up to the Wanderer and kissed him on both cheeks.

"I am Paulos."

"I am the Wanderer."

"May Jesus Christ be praised."

"To the Ages of Ages."

And each spoke in his own tongue, the crowd following each expression eagerly.

"What brings you here?" It was the Wanderer who spoke.

"I come to learn the news. And you?"

"The same."

Each spoke in his own language and each understood the other.

"Let there be contention," exclaimed one of the peasants suddenly.

"Contention. Contention," shouted all. For it was the custom in the Eastern lands and in the cities too, that when minstrels came together in any one place then there should be a contest and each should tell all he knew in order to outdo the other. The contests were usually entered into with friendliness on the part of both contestants but it often happened, particularly where some mischief-loving noble or burgomaster thrust in his oar, that the contest developed at length into a bitter battle. But in many cases it did not; it brought out friendly rivalry as in an athletic contest, each one of the participants attempting to outdo the other. When the news of the day had been exhausted the minstrels fell back upon verse of their own improvising; each one sometimes exhausted hours before his voice failed him and he allowed his rival an entry. In most cases, however, decency governed the contest and each minstrel would take only his allotted time and allow fair play to the other man.

And thus at the word "contest" both of the old men smiled, and yet looked down proudly upon their musical instruments. For much credit was to be gained in such contention; news of the contests often traveled ahead of the minstrels as they went from place to place, and he who could worst all rivals in verse, music, skill, upon his instrument, in wealth of anecdote, or in freshness of news, was always welcomed. Yet, many minstrels avoided such contests, particularly those who were of the lesser order of the craft. Here in this instance, however, were two seasoned veterans, both of them rich in years and experience, and both of them known and loved all over the Eastern lands.

The Wanderer raised his hand. A dead silence fell over the crowd. "Hear us, good people," he exclaimed. "We agree to the contest, but first you must fetch us food. To a good dog, a good home. We have traveled far and we have not eaten, and sweet music is no companion to hunger. Therefore we will eat what you provide, and thereupon will return to you all that you seek."

There was a rush for the cottages, for he was blest of God who fed a stranger, and he was all the more blest who fed a holy man, and these two old men seemed more like gods of olden time come across the steppe to bring good news in a troubled era. In a trice, it seemed, there was goat's milk, and dried meat—there was hard bread and fresh fruits. The two old men regaled themselves, exchanging anecdotes and news as they sat near each other —Michael eating with them and listening as if in a dream, and all tossing morsels of food to the little dog who danced about and wagged his stub of a tail.

# CHAPTER XII

## THE BATTLE OF THE MINSTRELS

WHEN the meal was eaten the two warriors drew themselves into position, the Wanderer upon the rock and Paulos upon the ground. It was quite evident to the spectators who looked on breathlessly that the Pole was granted the higher position because he had been first on the field; too, the other minstrel recognized the fact that the organistrum needed the full lap of the player on which to rest, whereas the harp could be played with the base upon the ground and the minstrel upon his knees by the side of it. A cloud suddenly rushed in front of the sun; it brought a change of mood in the two musicians apparently, for they were now no longer smiling. Friends though they were, by nature of their calling, this was to be a trial of skill and nerve. And it so happened that this was the first time that either had met in competition, and each knew the other as a master. The Wanderer was the minstrel monarch of the western steppes, the other the monarch of the east and south. A wind began to rise, the Wanderer raised his hand to his forehead and looked ahead abstractedly as if he saw into the unknown.

Then all at once he turned the lever and a musical note smote upon the air.

"I come," he chanted, as his fingers began to play with regularity upon the strings, the wheel revolving the while, "from the lands of the East:

> Tam jest wies Bahlaje
> Gdzie Czarny Szlak nastaje.

*Contest of the Minstrels*

(Lower border from one of the oldest peasant embroidery motives)

# THE BATTLE OF THE MINSTRELS

"There is the village of Bahlaje where begins the Czarny Szlak, the Black Trail.

"And over the Black Trail I have followed into the East. I have been over the Podolski Szlak, the Kuczmanski, by way of Trembovla and Zloczow. I have been over the Woloski Szlak from the South, and by it I came to Halich. Then I went down the Czarny Szlak through the Wolyn, and I came by Nikitma on the Dnieper. Then I went along the Kerman Yah which is the Turkish name for Caravan Road, and what I saw I saw."

"What did you see?" shrieked the peasants.

But the old man went ahead, without noticing the interruption. His hands were busy with his instrument, though slowly, for it was quite evident that he was only working into his theme by degrees. His voice came regularly and monotonously, the cadence was restrained—

"I saw—" he went on, "that along these old roads by which men once went south to the Krim to the Black Sea and to the old cities, I saw that by these roads there were coming people into Europe. Black, black, black were these roads—devastated with battle, blasted by fire, darkened with murder and theft and destruction; over them had ridden the Tartar horses tramping upon the soil until the grass itself became like night."

"We know. We know," they shouted.

"And in these lands the word has gone from mouth to mouth that a great prophecy has been fulfilled; that it has come the time for the East to triumph over the West. Men have waited day by day for this to happen, and now the people of the steppe are out on horses, the whole plain is moving, the nations are on the march. Suzdal is divided from Moskva, the Lithuanian from the Pole, the Greek from the Turk, and all are moving hither to Halich to fight the great battle which shall make these lands the lands of the East forever."

# THE GOLDEN STAR OF HALICH

And at that there fell upon the people a great fury of grief, for they realized then that these armies and horsemen coming upon Halich meant that a battle was to be fought before which all other battles were to pale.   Perhaps, they thought, it would be worse than in the times of Batu-Khan, when all those who lived in Halich and the Red Land were overcome by the Tartars; in those times no man had lived, save those who fled to Wengry or to Poland.

The sharp notes, softly blended, ceased to cut the air.

Then the other minstrel smote his harp.   "I come from the lands far to the south where Tsargrad raises its thousand spires. There in the city sit the emperor and his court and all are down-cast because the city is surrounded by enemies.   Around them rage the Turks—they have taken Asia Minor, they have swung back into the land of the Hellenes, and they have ploughed the land with fire and sowed it in salt.   But all about, the people are rising against the conquerors, and they say that if they had a leader they could drive back the infidel.   Now as I come up the broad stream of the Dniester in a galley draped in purple and gleaming with stars of the East, I hear the songs of the Greek rowers and I see the sun flash upon the arms of the Greeks and Bulgarians and men of Macedonia, and I know that war is to come.   Swiftly and like the lightnings, the clans will gather in Halich, and like the thunderbolts will they go forth and strike the Turks.   And then the land will be the land of the Roman Emperors again and there will be one ruler who will rule the whole."

He ceased and the harp was stilled.

It was now the Wanderer's turn and the eyes of all were upon him as he set his wheel in motion again.

"I am a Lech and I am come back here to see what will be the outcome of all this striving.   For the whole East is arrayed for battle. The whole Empire of the East sets itself up to flood our lands of the West. And here in Halich is the meeting. For do I not know that the Tartar has been summoned from Sarai to join these forces? That if the Khan chooses he may bring millions and millions of men to throw upon the Turks and so save the great Roman Empire of the East? And do I not know that there have gone to the great Khan, to Murut himself, the ambassadors—nay even the princes, the two Dimitris—he of Moskva and he of Suzdal? And do I not know that if the Khan chooses to set up Dimitri of Suzdal, then will the forces of the princes of Rus be joined with the boyars of Halich, and the soldiers of Greece will join with them? Have they not come to Halich in their galleys, and have they not jewels and gold and all that men desire?"

A silence fell over the crowd. Men and women looked into each other's eyes in grave astonishment. Could these things be?

The harpist took up the tale. "I am of the blood of Rus and through me runs the valor of Rurik and his Danes. I come from the East from the wilds of Dnieper, the steppes of the Don, the meadows of the Volga, even from the Tartar city of Sarai. And do I not know that the East will overcome the West, even as Kiev overcame Boleslas the Bold, and even as it overcame that other Boleslas who slew the saint at his own altar in Krakow? For we of the East think not of the day; there is all time ahead, and we shall array ourselves in fine purple and enjoy life while life is here to enjoy. And now we are come here to welcome our new ruler. A prophecy has come to pass. A new empire is rising. Out in the deserts and the wilderness there has arisen a Star. Men have looked for this Star for years; there hath been no greater Star since that day when the Great Star shone over the East and came to rest in Bethlehem. But this Star is not in the sky."

His hands were moving fast, his eyes were surging with emotion—his whole body was stiffening in the spell of his song.

"We of Rus will rule the world. We who live on the steppes

and travel by the great rivers, we will be the rulers of mankind. And with us will be the great East, and under us will be the Tartar and the Persian and the Turk and the Greek.  The Lith-uanian shall no more rule in the halls of ancient Kiev—in Nov-gorod, the Lord of cities, there shall be fear only of our own rulers, the Rus.  And Poland shall succumb to us, and the cities of the West.  And above all rulers in the world will be the Golden Star of Halich.  She it is who comes to us according to the prophecies. She it is beneath whose sway the proud Roman Empire of the East shall bow.  And there comes one than whom there is no greater monarch of the world, he the monk of Athos who comes to take the scepter again which men forced him to lay down.  He will rule beneath the Star, and Lev will rule beneath the Star, and the Tar-tar will fear the Star, and the Turk and the wild tribes of the steppe will flee before her armies. . . ."  He was deep in the trance, though his fingers plucked at the strings with twice the zeal that he had shown at the beginning—then all at once he ceased —his voice was raised and he was crying out, crying out as if in pain, "the Golden Star—the Golden Star—the Golden Star—" and then fell weak and fainting to the ground.

But the Wanderer seized his instrument and dashed forth chords from it that struck at the hearts of the men and women: "I am of the West.  I am a Lech, a Pole; and never across these steppes shall the armies of the East march into Christendom.  I can see the present and I see into the future and there I see my people standing like a wall against the hordes that sweep in from the East marching to destroy all that man has called his best civilization.  Across these steppes the battle cry is ringing, inva-sion after invasion, sword and fire, destruction and death, but still the Pole is standing on guard to drive back these invaders who come only to destroy.  I could not see clearly before, but now I can see, and I know that the West will ever hold its own.  Across

the plains of Asia I can see the horsemen urging on their steeds—
over these lands I can see them coming and the sun is hid by the
flight of arrows that their bowmen send up.  But here will we
stand upon this border, and here will we spend the blood which
God has given us; who may know what is right?  Who may
know what is best?  But we know what we have, we know what
blessings have been brought upon us by the light of day, and if
we are to be what God intended, then we must resist this East.
For I do not believe the old prophecy.  I do not know that the
East will win.  Tsargrad is mockery and corruption.  The Byzantine empire is crumbling in its own decay.  Suzdal is great but
Moskva is greater, and I know that the holy Alexis has himself
gone with the other Dimitri, the greater Dimitri, though yet a
boy, to Murut, and if he wins there, then will confusion fall upon
the Dimitri of Suzdal.  And I see the Lithuanian as one of the
West and not of the East—for in my sight I can see Christianity
spreading in that land, and I can see the waters of Christ drowning
the fires of Perkun."

He was at the height of his trance.  Fire blazed from his eyes.
His hair tossed in the wind.  "And I know too that this Golden
Star is not to be the ruler of these lands as you have said.  She is
naught but a simple girl, brought here to deceive men into believing
that an ancient prophecy has come to pass."

"Liar," shouted the harpist, rising to his feet.

"The truth."

"Liar."

"Then prove it."  The Wanderer rose as well.  The next instant they were in each other's arms, grappling.  The organistrum
descended upon the harp and there was a snapping of strings and a
smashing of wood.  They dropped the useless instruments and
rolled in the dirt, beating each other with their fists.  And around
them clustered in fright the peasants and Michael, the latter

holding the dog with all his might and main, for it was barking and almost screaming with eagerness to leap into the fray and help its master. . . . It was something more than an ordinary brawl, it was somehow as if two mountains with snow upon their crests had become alive and were grappling. They beat each other and tore at hair and beard, screaming the while.

And pandemonium it seemed was let loose in the town about them. Men and women shouted and dogs barked, children darted hither and thither among the spectators' legs, threatening to overturn people right and left. A flock of geese, pursued by a barefooted girl in bright-colored dress and headkerchief, ran directly into the crowd and fluttered here and there desperately, honking all the while, and striking out with long white necks and yellow bills. Some horses that were being led across one end of the fair ground became frightened and started to run away. The screaming increased, the excitement grew almost to a panic, when suddenly a great bell in a church high above their heads on the cliff began to ring. Crash-dong—Crash-dong—it went, then faster, and the crashing died out and only the reverberating was in the air. Dong-dong-dong—it sounded; not eastern tocsin nor western alarm bell could send such shivers down the spine as that bell.

The effect was magical. First of all the clamor seemed to bring the rival musicians to their senses.

"Enough, enough," shouted the Wanderer, leaping to his feet and brushing the dirt from his clothes. "There is enough honor for every man in this contest," and ecstatically he kissed the minstrel of Rus upon the cheeks.

"God be praised that I lived to this day," exclaimed the other, "for such improvising I never heard before."

And then embracing as if in the moment before they had not been engaged in a terrific battle, the old men kissed each other and tightened their girdles which had come unloosened in the fray.

"We will meet again," said the Wanderer.

"As brothers," said the other. And grasping at the remains of his harp he ran in the direction of the river.

The crowd now was melting fast, as over their heads the alarm bell kept up its tolling.

"My poor instrument," said the Wanderer ruefully. "I must needs go to Sambor for another frame. I know a man there who makes these of the best wood. And then I must take the frame to Lvov for the smith to fit with a wheel." So saying he tossed the remains of his battered organistrum behind the rock on which he sat.

"See how the crowd has dispersed," put in Michael.

"It is the alarm bell."

Most of the people had gone back to their houses, but a few, perhaps fifty, stood idly near one corner of the grounds looking about curiously as if anxious to see what the alarm foreboded. They had not long to wait, for around the end of the hill came sweeping a small company of horsemen in shining armor, their leader a tall man clad entirely in black.

"Why do you linger here?" he demanded at once of the crowd. "Have we not warned you to keep within your houses today?"

"We but came out to hear the minstrel," said one man, standing near.

"The minstrel, and where is he?"

They pointed. And as they pointed, the rider faced the old man and Michael; a terror clutched at Michael's heart for he saw that the rider was no other than Phokas the astrologer.

"So——" he exclaimed, "and the boy—why——" for though Michael had drawn back the hood over his head as fast as he was able, the astrologer's eyes were faster than his motion. "Take that boy," he screamed to two of his nearest men. "Seize him."

They dashed upon the little group, the minstrel, Michael, and the dog, but the band of peasants standing nearby were quicker than they. Sensing that wrong might come to the minstrel they leaped into a barrier before the oncoming horses and caught at the bridles.

"Out of the way," said the first rider, with an oath.

"Touch not our minstrel. He is a holy man. He is of God," exclaimed the peasants. And in defence of his person it was likely that they would have died. For in most things the peasant was humble and lowly, he was a worm before soldiers and was called "stinker" in the dialect of Rus, so little did men of the upper classes regard him. But in the defence of his shrines and his prophets, the peasant was ever willing to die. So had it been in Kiev, and Novgorod, so was it to be in Vilno and Chenstohova. And in defence of the minstrel they were prepared to give their lives.

Now had the leader kept his head and explained to the peasants that he did not want the minstrel, but only the boy, then it is possible that he might have obtained him; possible, though perhaps he might have been obliged to overrule objections on the part of the minstrel. But he lost his head entirely at sight of Michael, for news of the sinking galley had reached him, and he had believed that the boy was lost; to see him now, probably on the way to the Duke to expose him, was more than he could endure. And so he rushed on, his horse knocking down two men and stepping upon another.

This stirred up the hornets' nest. "Drag them from their horses"—"They would strike the man of God"—"Kill"—"Slay" —such expressions rose from their lips as they threw themselves upon the riders. In a moment two of the leader's men were unhorsed, and the sound of staves striking home added to the clamor of the bell which was continuing its alarm. But the attack upon Michael had been diverted.

"Come," said a peasant, dragging at the old man and the boy in great haste, "you must escape from here. I will take you to the edge of the stream where there is a boat." Michael at first thought that he meant the Dnieper, and his heart sank at the idea that he was fleeing from Halich after all, but he soon realized that the man meant the Lukiev, since they had left the town houses and were scurrying, through ruins overgrown with bushes, in a westerly direction. The town quickly fell away behind, the noise died out, and sheltered by low trees and decaying brick walls they reached the edge of the stream and saw a long, crude boat held to the shore beneath some overhanging trees.

"Get in the boat and pull upstream," said the peasant. "You will soon be out of danger's reach."

Overjoyed that here was the quickest and best way to reach the castle at Krylos, Michael leaped into the boat and was followed by the old man and the dog. Thrusting the hand-made oars into the water he pushed away from the shore and found that progress was easy in the gently flowing stream. Their rescuer stood upon the bank and waved to them as long as they could see, but at length a slight curve in the river hid him from their sight.

# CHAPTER XIII

## THE CORONATION

FOR two or three hours the boy rowed steadily, keeping the little craft well within the shadow of trees on the shore. The old minstrel seated in the bow slept. His venerable head was tilted forward, his hands folded. The little dog, companion of all his joys and woes, also slept—lying at his feet, curled up, he wakened from time to time and glanced up at his master, but seeing him motionless went back to another period of sleep. The river itself was not deep here, but in ancient times the Halichians had dug out the mud in the bottom and widened the channel. When Michael rowed up it that day it was already showing signs of becoming what later it did become, a small, shallow stream; the soil was washing from the hills into the channel, the water was settling to new, narrower banks, and verdure was springing up where once there had been water.

Well it was that he had eaten and recruited his strength, for now, in the current, it was no small task to keep the boat steadily upstream. However, the current was not swift, and there was no reason for hurry, once the town had been left behind. The afternoon waned, the dusk crept upon them slowly, the red sky turned to purple and to gray—they came around one last bend in the stream, and there before their eyes the towers of the Halich castle and Cathedral rose majestically in the air.

"Wake," exclaimed Michael, shooting the boat to shore and drawing in his oars. "We are here."

# THE CORONATION

The minstrel rose, heavy with sleep, and followed him as he leaped to shore. "We will wait by those trees until it is dark, and then we will make our way to the gate. I am sure that the guard will know me and lead me to the Duke."

Now the position of the old grod, Halich, was as near perfection in the matter of being a well-fortified citadel as might be found in any country in the world. It lay upon a high piece of land, shaped like a human tongue, protected on three sides by water and marshy land; on the fourth, the southwest, ably defended by natural ridges of land which cut off the lower end of the peninsula from the upper end. Over this height of land rose the ruins of the palaces of the old druzina. Near the northern extremity, about halfway from either end of the peninsula, stood the castle of the grand duke; it was of stone below and wood above, and at the time of Michael's imprisonment there was practically a new structure built upon the ruins of the other castle. Adjoining this castle, or rather serving as the great central building of the castle group, was the enormous stone structure, the Cathedral, with its two defence towers, its separate walls and its gates.

At the lower end of the peninsula was the old Halich gate, by which one entered from the drawbridge over the little stream Mozoliev which, running through swampy ground, joined the River Lukiev at a point close to the bank where Michael had pulled in his boat.

They waited under the trees, the minstrel musing, Michael thinking. Once when the boy looked at the older man he saw that tears stood out upon his cheeks, and thinking that perhaps the minstrel had suffered injury in the fight asked him gently:"Is there some way in which I may help you?"

"No," said the minstrel, ashamed that someone had seen his weakness. "I but wept for that which had kept me company all these years, but is now broken and destroyed upon the Halich

[ 167 ]

plain.   From east to west, from north to south we have wandered together, and the strings upon it knew my voice as well as I knew its song.   However, it died gloriously, in a battle between the East and West, and there is another to be made in Sambor. . . . But look," he exclaimed, leaping to his feet and pointing out over the plain, "see, the whole earth is alight."

Michael looked.   And indeed it seemed as if the minstrel's words were true.

For as far as he could see, and it was now growing darker and darker, the entire plain of the old kingdom was lighted up by the glare of torches.

"There must be thousands of men there," declared the minstrel.

"Indeed there must," replied the boy.

And truly the whole place seemed to be astir.   Whence these troops had come so suddenly it was impossible to conjecture.   But there they were on the farther side of the River Lukiev, company after company of them, and they were all on the march toward the castle as could be seen from the movement of the torches.

"Come," said Michael," we will enter the castle by this gate."

They crossed the swamp carefully on the remains of what had once been a road, but now was merely a rough footpath with boggy places to right and left.   Just before reaching the gate, this path swung into the main road leading from the left through the gate.   And as they came out from behind a jutting elbow of rock to join the main road, all about them became suddenly as light as day.   The earth was shaking with the tread of marching men, and music from trumpets was setting the cadence which they all followed.

It was too late to retreat; they hurried to the roadside and threw themselves into a company of townfolk that was following the troops.   They passed unnoticed until they reached the gate of the ducal city, where curiously enough the guards seemed to be refraining from duty, and letting the crowds pass through without question. Thus the two advanced with the marching multitude into the grod, and began the ascent of the road to the Cathedral. And there was something in the air that thrilled them through and through. The marching multitude, the glaring torches that roared and snapped with red flame and smoke—the bells were sounding now from the Cathedral, and the trumpets still kept up their fanfare. And to add to this, certain groups of soldiers began to sing, making the music fit the rhythm of their steps.

Michael's first and greatest impulse was to find his way to the Duke, but he saw, as they marched, that this was impossible. The best thing that he could do would be to keep with the others and step forward to make his way to the Duke whenever there came a chance.

But that chance never came. Yet, when the procession had reached the gate leading between the towers to the Cathedral, the marching men halted, and only those who were leading them went inside the gate. Drawn up in company outside were the tribes of North and South in leather accouterments, and as if acting as guards of honor at the gate were Greeks in shining armor of black and white. But between their two lines were advancing to the church door the captains and chiefs clad in magnificent trappings—gold and silver and purple, their swords adorned with precious metals and glittering gems.

"Wait here till I rejoin you," said Michael, suddenly, throwing off the outside garment which the minstrel had given him, and appearing in the splendid, though water-stained, garments bestowed upon him by the Duke. "I am going inside."

Just then a burst of music from the Cathedral fell upon the ears of the men outside. It was a chorus singing a triumphal song; and at the moment when men's attentions were caught by it, Michael shot out from the side of the gate and walked swiftly and

unostentatiously through with the marching chieftains.  His garments, though water-stained, were of undeniable richness; under
ordinary circumstances he might perhaps have been held up and
questioned, but his own agility and the rather uncertain torch-light
aided him.  In an instant he was inside the huge portals which
arched in a curve above him—a series of variously designed arches,
five or six of them, as if one were built inside the other, with the
outer arch inclosing above the door a huge tableau of the Annunciation.

Then there broke upon his eyes such a scene of splendor as he
had never witnessed before.

Hanging lamps and huge candles lit up the richly adorned interior of the Cathedral, illuminating almost every inch of space
and bringing into relief the magnificent mosaics upon the wall and
the down-looking face of God high up in the central dome.  In
the midst of this splendor of scene, where all the assembled company were in a mood of rapture or admiration, Michael slipped
forward unperceived past a line of pillars that set off the central
nave upon the left, and took a position near the front of the Cathedral where he could see all that transpired.  He had a pillar
at his back in this position, and in front of him the rich ikonostasis
or screen which hid the Great Altar.

For the Halich Cathedral was an echo of the magnificent ca-
thedrals that rose in Byzantium when the Eastern Roman Empire
was at its height of influence.  From west to east a broad nave
swept through the building; the flanking aisles were broad spaces
in themselves, set off by rich, fluted pillars.  In three apses of
the Cathedral, toward which the aisles and nave pointed, were
the three altars, the altars to the saints lying at the head of the
aisles; the main or Great Altar, which was the altar of the Sacrament, standing at the head of the nave in an apse larger than the
other two, and shut off by the ikonostasis or screen.  But be-

tween the place where the aisles and naves ended, and the place where the altars stood beneath the curving apse walls, rose a huge tower—a very series of arches, crowning each other tier on tier, until at length they ended in a sharp six-faced brick framework like a collar, above which was a slightly rounding dome.

Michael saw with bewilderment that not one inch of this space was free from adornment. Where the rounding arches rose on the first tier to support the second tier were four angels in red and gold, and above them between the windows of the hexagon were Moses and Jacob, and Isaac and David. Woven in bricks of gold and white and blue were these faces,—each face a composite of tiny cubes that made up the whole picture. And all about the church were pictures from the Old and New Testaments in the same marvelous design. Here in one was the Patriarch of Constantinople offering a Cathedral to Our Lord who sat upon a throne. Here was an angel with the words of the Annunciation, and marvelously designed was the Virgin with the walls of her home, and the well beside it. Mosaics of all the colors of the rainbow—pictures designed of tiny blocks that ran into the thousands in forming one complete scene. And in the lights thrown upon them, the images seemed ethereal and unearthly.

Then he looked about upon the company. Truly the lords of the earth were here in all their magnificence.

For ranged against the sumptuous background of pillar, brick wall of yellow and blue, mosaic, stained glass—were men of all the nations of the East: the lines of Greek officers in black and white armor—the mail coats, hanging loosely to the knees, caught at the waist where a short, wide sword went through the belt—the knees and legs encased in metal down to the pointed toes and spurred heels, the narrow shields, the helmets rising to a point; the Lithuanians, masters of the old Rus lands from the Baltic to the Black Sea, in leather garments reinforced with metal and over

THE GOLDEN STAR OF HALICH

their shoulders the skins of wild beasts; the Bulgarians in shining silver armor; the Tartars, thin and lithe, with pointed helmets, round shields, and glittering with golden ornament; boyars of Rus and of Suzdal with the short battle axes of the Slav, with purple armor and long swords; Hungarians and Czechs were there in the new armor of the West, thick metal plates with joints at elbow and knee, casques with pointed visors. These and other leaders the boy saw as he gazed.

And then all at once the whole Cathedral burst into song, the choir, ranged at the rear, and beyond the dome to the right and the left in what might be termed the transept in a Western church, burst into a chant of triumph. The center of the church was cleared by boys in the vestments of the Church carrying the censers full of smoking coals; behind them came a procession of courtiers carrying on a huge platform a great ivory throne. The platform and the throne were placed before the ikonostasis, not far from the place where Michael was standing. And then, as at a signal, the Metropolitan himself appeared at the Gospel door of the ikonostasis, and at the Epistle door was his deacon, and the chant took on the cadence of a processional, for a great company was advancing through the space cleared by the acolytes.

Michael gazed at the throne. It was indeed the symbol of royalty. Carved out of ivory, it stood some six feet high, resting upon four crouching lions of some yellow metal like to gold—perhaps gold—and in itself a marvel of tracery. The high back rose to a point and upon the crest was a crown, fashioned by some goldsmith centuries before, with jewels standing out in relief upon it. In front of the throne richly dressed pages brought a purple carpet and over the platform surface were laid cushions of purple and gold.

But the coronation procession was advancing, led by a second

choir of youths, in red and white vestments—no instrumental
music fell upon the ear for in the Church of the East that music
was forbidden; at their head was a crucifer and the cross with
the two cross-pieces, the lower to designate our Lord's agony
upon the cross, for in the Eastern Church there must be no figure
of Our Lord designed—instead the symbol of His suffering is
the lower cross-piece, the limb which lay across the wood. The
first choir was now silent, waiting for the response—this second
choir had begun a hymn of praise.

Behind the choir came the priests who were beneath the Metropolitan in rank, all of them in rich vestments; behind the priests
came the nobles. As the procession made its way through the
Cathedral it divided at the throne, and those who were part of
it stood about the throne in two groups. The lesser chiefs fell
back to the farther parts of the church or into the two side aisles.
Michael held his place by struggling vigorously. Part of the
procession had come to a halt directly before him, but he was fortunate in that he could see between two boys of the choir.

Surging still farther came the others of that procession: in
the lead was an old monk in brown cassock; behind him came
Duke Lev and the leaders of the forces which were then encamped
upon Halich. The Tartar and the Lithuanian seemed stiffly awk-
ward and ill at ease in that company; for the Lithuanian was a
pagan, and the Tartar a disciple of Mohammed, and the church
of Christians was to them a forbidden place.

The whole company now came to a halt, the nobles ranging
themselves to left and right about the throne, leaving a space for
one to enter between their ranks and take seat upon it. At
length the one came—the chant rose to the roof, the colors swam,
the smoking incense pots threw shadows in the boy's eyes—it was
Katerina, in a long robe of white silk, held up by two pages—her

eyes were downcast, and upon her face was an expression of fear and anxiety that betokened great pain; her golden hair was caught in a simple band of gold behind.

She seated herself upon the throne, rested her head upon her right hand, her elbow upon the ivory support that formed the arm of the throne, and almost immediately the Metropolitan's voice rose in a chant, and the choir thundered a response. One by one the clergy went into the sanctuary, the voice of the Metropolitan rose high and alone above their voices, and the service of the Coronation was sung. And when he appeared at the Gospel door the clergy flung themselves upon their knees, and the prayer, as if inclosed in the clean white fragrance of incense, rose through the roof to the skies.

The service continued until, at one juncture, the Metropolitan came forth from the sanctuary bearing in his hand a small crown of gold. To the throne he advanced, and she, the Golden Star, came forward and knelt before him. With words that winged their way into every corner of the edifice he placed the crown upon her head and kissed her upon either cheek; and almost simultaneously the choirs burst into one great hymn of thankfulness so that the windows rattled at the sound. And then, the Metropolitan retiring, there came boys with tablets and hyacinth ink, and with a huge quill and trembling hand she signed the tablets that recorded her oath. And having done so, she arose, the Empress of the Eastern World.

And at once the voice of the Metropolitan rose over the shouts of acclaim that swept the Cathedral, calling for the oaths of loyalty by the leaders who stood about the throne.

The priest in the brown habit stepped forward. Dramatically throwing off the brown robes he stood before them in the garb of an emperor; he was an old man though vigorous, with beard and drooping moustache once jet black but now turning white. Upon

*Coronation of the Golden Star*

(Details from "Ewangelicka Ormianska" Armenian Gospel, 1198 A.D.; capitals
from fragments found on Krylos Hill.)

THE CORONATION

his head was a regal miter of silk and gold to serve as a crown, his robe was of purple, with embroidered hem and collar; and designs of slanting lines in the form of a cross were woven across the lace panel of his robe. Upon his feet were red buskins.

"I give my oath," he said in a voice that stabbed the ears, "to the Golden Star of Halich. For I, the monk Joasaph, am that John Kantakuzene, emperor of the Roman Empire of the East. From the cloister I come to see the resurrection of that empire. For he who sits upon its throne is but a careless spectator of the public ruin. All about, the Turks have encompassed the land. Christians are sold as slaves in the marts of Constantinople, churches are made into mosques, villages and cities of its domains are pillaged. I would have saved them had they wished, but they chose to follow that one who rules them, that one who bears my own name. Thousands and thousands of my subjects, bearing arms and possessing gold, stand ready all through the Empire to revolt against the conqueror. And it is beneath Your Rule that we will conquer, for while you rule the Eastern lands from Halich I will again rule my own lands of Rome."

Duke Lev came forward, and knelt before the throne: "And I will rule the land of Halich."

The Tartar came forward and extended his right hand, not kneeling, for was he not the Tartar monarch of the Slav lands? "We will be brothers and drive out the Turks and Poles," he said.

An ambassador from Olgerd, the Lithuanian, approached and fell upon one knee: "And we, too, will serve with thee against the Turk and the Pole, and if need be against the enemies of the realm."

And then came a Bulgarian, men of Rus from Suzdal, others of the tribes of the East.

A huge confederation! And held together by one bond, the Golden Star—Lev was hoping to regain the domain of the boyars,

[ 175 ]

# THE GOLDEN STAR OF HALICH

John Kantakuzene the land of the Byzantines, the Rus, of Suzdal, the grand dukedom of the East; the Tartars had booty and
gold yet to win, the Lithuanian could extend his conquest to east
and west by this confederation.  The Golden Star was the emblem—for did not a prophecy of old tell of the coming of the
Star when the nations should unite and the greatest confederation
of empires known to man should come into existence?  And yet
did not all realize how desperate the chance?  For a single
breath might bring the whole structure down.

And now a tall figure in white silk has come before the throne;
it is Phokas the astrologer, and well concealed in the crowd behind
him is the dwarf, in black silk, leering, with huge head and grin-
ning mouth, and a dagger at his belt.

"I come," said Phokas, "to tell what the Heavens have de-
creed.  We are assembled in the House of Lev, of Leo, the Lion,
the sign which dominates the Heavens in the late summer, for it
is in that House that the sun now dwells. . . .  And he who now
shall rule the land of the Lion is the Lion himself. . . .  He was
born," indicating the Duke, "in this very House of the sun.  The
star which dominates that House is Regulus, and Regulus is a
king. . . .  The star is purple, and purple is the sign of kingship.
For of all the Houses that are found in the Mazzaroth, that of the
Lion is the greatest.  But the sun itself is the star which carries
his fortunes; gold is the metal which is the highest and best and
therefore of that house; the topaz which gleams in his helmet is
the stone that will bring him fortune, and his vital element is
blood, blood and power."

He paused: all in the assembly were breathless, and awed almost
to the point of falling upon their knees.  Phokas continued.
"Therefore when it was resolved by us that beneath the House
of Lev we should assemble, I searched the Heaven for signs and
found that all were favorable.  And in so many ways were there

signs that Heaven itself had decided for this leader, that we made this our one attempt. He was born beneath a royal star, and now the sun is in the House of that star.

"And the time is now ripe to conquer the Turks. Shall we march?"

"We shall!" It was shouted through the church and men drew out their swords.

"When?"

"Now," the cry rose to the roof and broke into a thousand echoes.

"Then we go."

From outside there came the sound of men marching. It seemed as if the whole world of the East were in motion.

But suddenly the motion ceased as if by magic. Some threatening stillness fell upon the multitude. Outside the Cathedral there was no more sound than exists in a tomb; inside a silence leaped out of somewhere and descended upon the chiefs.

"What is this?" exclaimed Phokas.

Michael looked at Emperor John Kantakuzene and Duke Lev, who stood side by side at the right of the astrologer. Some shadow had crossed their faces, driving away the expression of triumph that had been there but a few moments before. And from the rear door of the Cathedral, near which men were now drawing aside to let some one pass, there came a murmur of doubtful voices.

A messenger in the garb of a herald came forcing his way through the crowd.

"News, I bring news," he exclaimed. And bowing to all he delivered his message aloud—he was a youth, and he had ridden far, for his clothes were splashed with mud and here and there showed rents.

"I come from Olgerd the Lithuanian. He has this day resolved to make no war upon the Poles, with whom he has an alliance of friendship and blood."

There was silence again, and he bowed low, and then, as if sensing the unwelcome effects of his message, walked straight for the Cathedral door and disappeared through it. And after him went the Lithuanian envoy, and outside one could hear the Lithuanian soldiery moving along the road in preparation for departure.

Duke Lev grew pale, but Kantakuzene smiled. "What need have we of the Lithuanians?" he asked. "They are but few in number, although very warlike, and have perhaps risen to power only through the valor of their leaders and the weakness of their enemies."

"It is true," answered the Duke, "although I had counted upon them."

The murmuring in the church increased as two more messengers made their way to the ivory throne.

"Here come the men that I expected," said Duke Lev. "I sent them with instructions to return tonight with news from our allies. They are my own men and bring, I know, tidings of success."

The first messenger bowed low, then began falteringly:

"I come from Suzdal where I have been in the house of Dimitri, and the news that I bring is bad. For your ally, Dimitri of Suzdal, has been beaten in his claims for the grand dukedom of All the Russias. The grand dukedom has passed to Dimitri of Moskva, with whom the Hòly Alexis went to the Tartar Khan, Murut. And for this, the men of Rus will not serve in the armies of the Golden Star. The once hostile Dimitris are now united in love and alliance." And the messenger withdrew in trembling.

"Now we are lost," exclaimed the Duke, "for with the men of Rus will go the Tartars."

[ 178 ]

And at this the other messenger made his report: "What you say is true, Duke Lev," he reported. "The Khan Murut has decided that none must occupy the ducal throne save Dimitri of Moskva; and he orders his Tartars who are here to withdraw. With them will go all the tribes of the steppe."

"And the Bulgarians," came the voice of a leader in the Cathedral.

And in a moment Michael saw that the whole conspiracy, hatched with so much care, was broken like an egg tossed from a cliff. Bound together with light bonds, fantastic almost in its conception, the plot was dependent upon all these elements, and now, not by the direct agency of man but by some influence of chance, the scheme was broken just as it was made. And looking at the faces of these men who had planned so much—Kantakuzene, a well-disposed and valorous man—he who wished to save his ancient country from the Turks, Duke Lev, the last of the Boyars of Halich, who had believed that upon the crumbling remains of an ancient city he could once more erect a powerful empire—upon the faces of these men he saw written a bitter sadness. There was no anger nor fear—that which to them had been the great issue of their lives was simply overthrown, ended, in an instant. Not so with Phokas. For he, alarmed, and mindful of his own safety, was already shouting out orders to his Greeks—there were perhaps five hundred of them altogether—for it was quite evident that in a moment the army assembled under Halich would break up into many and hostile parts. Indeed the shouts of the Tartars, informed of the news, outside, were rising in increasing violence.

"Quick. Shut the gates to the Cathedral—" the command came from Phokas. "When the chiefs have returned to their men, bar the door behind them. We must fight if we are to get out of this alive."

And indeed the place was one of confusion. Men were tumbling over each other in the rush to the doors—all, save the Greek soldiery and a few boyars who gathered about Lev, were intent on saving themselves. These too, with Kantakuzene, moved finally to the great doors, leaving the church deserted except for the priests, and the girl who sat in terror upon the ivory throne. For in all that confusion, not even Lev had thought of her; so occupied were all with the news and so perturbed to see its effects upon the gathered armies. The Duke finally broke away from his men and came bounding back to lead her away from the throne, but not before Michael had come out from behind his pillar and rushed up to her.

"Michael," she said, and the color flashed into her pale cheeks. "Michael. I am frightened—but I am glad." And she came down from the throne and gathered up the train of her dress, for the pages who bore it into the Cathedral had fled with the rest. The Duke came up to her at this moment, with a quick command: "To your room and change your dress, for we must be ready to ride at any moment." And in an instant they were gone, although she did look back and smile at the boy while her father was leading her away.

Swiftly the Metropolitan and his priests gathered up the glories of the coronation, the crown which had been upon the girl's head, the rich robes, the banners, and the crosses; and then several men came in and slid the throne out a side door, on rollers; the candles were burning low and bulging in their sockets; acolytes were extinguishing the glow in the lamps; finally only the red light showed where the Sacrament was upon the altar. The priests came through the sanctuary doors clad now in black, and, kneeling and kissing the holy picture in front of the ikonostasis, departed by the same exit where the throne had gone. Michael stumbled in the semi-darkness for the rear door; a terrific silence had now fallen

# THE CORONATION

upon the Cathedral but through the stained glass windows there was now coming in from the outside the red glare of torches and burning buildings, and a great clamor of shouts and screams was rising in the air.

# CHAPTER XIV

## THE STORMING OF KRYLOS

AS he came out into the air, all about him was lurid in the dark yellow glare. Behind him the Cathedral and the palace were in darkness; through the gate on the front, however, between the two towers, could be seen a very sea of torchlights, extending along the road to the Halich gate, and down across the River Lukva to the plain. The plain, where the houses of the old city had been, was also aglow, and here and there red flames were curling up through the thatches of peasant houses, for the Tartar forces were unleashed at last and terror and death stalked boldly on every hand. Down in the new town the villagers had built a rapid barricade, and led by the hetman were prepared to die in defence of their homes.

This then was the situation as Michael saw it. The Tartar chiefs with the tribal leaders, the Polovtsy and others, had gone back through the Halich gate to their men and given the order to commence plundering. The few Bulgarians and Greeks brought by Kantakuzene were grouped about the yard inside the court, bordered by the walls and towers, with the Cathedral at their back. The few boyars of Halich were attempting to hold the Halich gate, and had sent another detachment to guard the German gate at the southern approach. The Lithuanians and men of Suzdal were taking no part in the uproar, but were being marshaled by their men across the bridge at the new village and were preparing to march away. They at any rate would not unite against Duke Lev and the Greeks as yet.

But it was the Tartar army spread out in battle array that promised to make trouble, and they were by far the greatest unit in the assembled company. They had had enough sight of the riches of the Cathedral, of the wealth brought by the Greeks, and of the men and women assembled there who might become slaves, to drive them on to plunder and rapine. And the enforced discipline which had lain over them for so many days, and their presence in a land which was their natural prey—these factors turned their passive obedience to a hot desire for plunder. Their ire fell first upon the peasants who were luckless enough to be near them, and then they marshaled themselves to take the Cathedral, the palace, and all the occupied houses.

Phokas, dashing through the court, sought Kantakuzene. "We must escape by the galleys," he shouted. "There is still a passage through the woods to the Dniester." He was in great trepidation, not for his liege, but for himself; he would have deserted all and fled willingly had he not known that the officers left in the galleys would not leave Halich without their master, and he knew also that the nobles in Tsargrad who had sent him would swiftly hang him for a traitor should he return without the former emperor. But in his swift reasoning there was room for reproach, reproach of Kantakuzene for inspiring his followers in a mad plan, reproach of himself for being such a fool as to come upon this errand. Till now he had looked out for himself; now all must escape together or perish together.

But Michael looking out to the East saw that the escape on that side was impossible; the Tartar cavalry had already occupied the old road. And they were making no secret of their movements either, for already captured peasants were running ahead of the horses carrying lighted torches to show the path.

# THE GOLDEN STAR OF HALICH

Duke Lev, with his druzina, and Kantakuzene emerged from the palace at this moment and surveyed the scene before them. "We are caught in here!" exclaimed the former emperor. Then he called to the astrologer. "Phokas. . . . There is no escape possible by the boats."

"There is unless they are burnt," shouted back the astrologer. "I gave orders to the rowers to keep away from land, awaiting orders. Could we but hold off this attack for an hour we could make the boats in safety."

"And is there no way?"

"There is," said the astrologer. "Krok—Krok—Krok," he shouted.

The dwarf came hurrying out of the shadows.

"Mount that tower on the left, and at the word, place fire upon the tubes. I shall be in the right tower and will fire first. You can hear me as I shout."

"What is your plan?" asked Kantakuzene.

"This. I have the hollow tubes which have been used in Germany—the invention perhaps of an Englishman. In these tubes I have placed Chinese powder. The tubes are filled with stone and scraps of iron. When fire is applied they will explode and deluge the oncoming Tartars with missiles. Thus I hope to hold them up for a short time. While the Tartars retreat, as retreat they must at first, then you and your company can make a dash for the path leading to the river and we will follow. Once aboard there is nothing to fear."

Then, it seemed to Michael, the uproar became clamorous. Had his life at Krylos up to that time been unreal, with men and women passing before him like the puppets of a Christmas show or *szopka,* now that life became a dream—a fragment of unreality that burned with the intensity of flame. Something suddenly nosed his leg—he reached down and touched the cold nose of a

[ 184 ]

little dog, and almost at once the old minstrel stepped out from the shadow of the gate.

"It has come," he said—"out there is an enemy that surrounds us. May I live to sing the story of this battle!"

The boy stroked the trembling dog and embraced the master. And then there came running to them Katerina, in the same riding habit that she had worn on the day when they escaped the brigands in the Church of St. Pantalemon.

"It is the Golden Star," he said to the minstrel, seizing both of the girl's hands. She turned to the old man, her face alight with emotion—pale no longer though the yellow light inclined one's complexion to paleness.

He stepped back to survey her. But before he had spoken there came an immense shout from the Halich gate. Duke Lev, striding across the court, leaped upon his horse which stood there, called to his men to follow, and rode straight down the road to the gate. Kantakuzene with a detachment of Greeks circled the Cathedral, and gathered on the natural fortifications at the German gate—the archers and spearmen on the tops of the mounds, the horsemen down below waiting for a charge or for an attack if the gate were broken down.

The old man with the boy on one side, the girl on the other, and the dog following, advanced to a position just outside the entrance to the Cathedral court where they could see plainly the main attack. At this point the Tartars were divided into three groups, all focusing on the gate. The cavalry were on the main road, archers and infantry on the left, and at the right a picked body of mounted and unmounted men ready to rush the gate when the signal came. Some carried huge axes. Piles of lumber standing about to be used in the rebuilding of Krylos had been robbed of their toughest and stoutest beams, and these, carried by dozens of men, were ready to be thrown into position for battering rams.

A trumpet sounded somewhere and the attack was on. Simultaneously it came, from front and rear, the boyars at the Halich gate, the Greeks at the German gate. Arrows showered down upon the defenders, the men at the gate drove forward with the rams, and a wild shouting and yelling rent the air. Though outnumbered ten to one and even more, the defenders had the advantage of the natural fortification and the shelter of the reconstructed gates and walls; yet the horsemen on the side of the Halich gate were powerless and finally descended from their horses, for there was not enough room to deploy, and the main work was the repelling of the besiegers.

Suddenly the Halich gate burst into flame, and from the attackers came a cry of triumph. They had approached close enough on the west side to hurl huge quantities of Greek fire upon it, and the flames mounting swiftly ran up the sides, and drove away the defenders who had kept their position there hurling spears or stones upon the Tartars. The archers, who had been dealing death from the defensive wall close beside the gate, were also driven back, and it gave the attackers room to drive the rams into the woodwork. They crashed there again and again, and finally the fiercely burning timbers began to drop. There was an opening—the sparks leaped high as the advance line fighting like demons forced the boards aside and plunged through. Here they met the stone wall of the defence, Duke Lev with his men stretched across the narrow roadway, their swords cutting and hacking, and the men on either side of them swinging their huge axes.

"Forward," went up the Tartar order, the officers beating their soldiers with whips, and like the stream that pours through a broken dam the stream of attackers surged through the gap in the defence. And now the cavalry dashed in behind the infantry, and the force drove down upon the Halich boyars.

"Retreat," commanded Duke Lev, "but retreat in order, until we come to the gates of the Cathedral." They fell back, fighting every inch of the way, until the towers at the Cathedral gate loomed over their heads.

Michael, the old man, and Katerina fell back inside the gates with the soldiers. The girl clung to them both as if for protection though she had shown no fear in all the tumult, save that she had trembled lest something befall her father at the gate. They took refuge behind a buttress flanking the tower, where no spear nor arrow from beyond the gate could reach them.

And then in a moment when it seemed as if a lull came in the clashing of arms, she looked up at Michael and said: "Michael— I wonder if we can come from all this alive?"

The boy looked around. "I feel somehow that we shall. I don't know why, but it is part of my feeling. Then besides—"

"What?" she asked.

"It may be that my father will come with the King's troops."

"With the King's troops—but Michael, how does he know?"

"I sent for him. The Tsigan carried my message."

Hope lit up her face. "Then, Michael, it may be that there is a chance—"

"It may be. . . . But—how different it will be. The plans have failed, your father may be a fugitive, and you yourself will no longer be the ruler of these lands."

"Michael, I could shout my thanks for that until the Tartars heard me. You know how unwillingly I submitted to all this; you know it was because of my father's wishes, and because he was so intent, and because he was my father I obeyed him."

"But your father will be Duke no longer."

"Michael, I am even thankful for that. I think that it was but a dream, this dukedom, for there are no more boyars now, save those few who help him. The land is the land of the Poles—

[ 187 ]

they have defended it from the Tartar and they were here in the early days when they were driven out by Vladimir. Michael, I myself am Polish at heart. I was brought up in Poland, in the church of the West, and all these things of the East are barbarous to me."

"It is curious," he said, "how no one thought of you after the messengers came with the bad news."

"I do not matter to them. I am but a symbol. I am only the sign. I was never anything else. . . . But, Michael, may your father come in time!"

"That I hope."

"And how can he reach us if the Tartars hold the bridge? They will burn it if troops try to cross."

"The townfolk are holding it now. It may be that word has reached them that the Poles are coming."

"May they come in time—may they come in time," she prayed.

But now inside the court all was action. The gates between the towers had been slammed and fastened with huge timbers, and the men mounting to the walls were again shouting defiance at the Tartars, and the archers were sending down a storm of arrows. Duke Lev had mounted to a high place over the gate and in the face of flying arrows and missiles was giving commands.

Then suddenly from the rear of the Cathedral came loud shouts. The Tartars had broken down the new-placed German gate and had driven the Greeks with Kantakuzene within the walls which protected the Cathedral. At the rear the defences were not so high nor so strong; perhaps in the old days they had been stronger, for when Koloman and Salomea took refuge here against the boyars they had held out for many days. Now the retreating Greeks were not able to stem the tide at the defence walls, and were obliged to take refuge within the Cathedral itself, barring the

[ 188 ]

doors and shooting down at the attackers from the narrow windows.

But on the front side where Duke Lev with his boyars held off the most powerful attack, the inner defence wall and gate still held. The Tartars had not brought up the beams from below, where the Halich gate had been demolished, and it would take some time to convey them up the hill to the Cathedral gate. However, a great body of men were at work transporting them, and in the gleam of torches the Tartars swarmed like ants over the whole promontory of land. Once Michael mounted one of the inner wall supports and looked down upon the ghastly scene; as far as he could see, the Tartar helmets shone yellow in the light; faces of hideous lineament, black pointed beards, narrow, squinting eyes—all these seemed like some impossible nightmare. But still they came on like the waves of the sea.

"We shall be engulfed," he thought, "before aid comes." But hope came to him as he thought of the stout-hearted villagers defending the lower roads. "They will fight until they die."

And now once more there came a new attack; the cavalry were rushing forward up the narrow road, packing it densely with fighting men and driving the foot soldiers ahead against the gate. It was hideous warfare, and warfare that took little count of the lives of friend or foe; Michael could see the object—that by the force of numbers and by the weight of bodies piling upon the Cathedral gates, they were soon likely to fall. Greek fire, however, availed little here; the boyars were on the watch and shot down with arrows all those who bore the flaming stuff nearby, and besides, the gates here were ancient and not new-made, and flames spread only with difficulty upon surfaces such as these where the metal embossing was heavy. But the horde was pressing upon the woodwork with terrific force, and the pressure was increas-

ing with every second, as the cavalry behind drove the foot soldiers ahead.

But all at once the whole situation was changed. As long as
the defence party had the Cathedral behind them, they felt rather
secure; but when the Greeks driven from the German gate began
to retreat through the Cathedral, it seemed for the time as if
the Tartars would close in on all sides. However, the small
doors on the lower side of the Cathedral prevented a rush from
that quarter, and besides the walls were of stone and it would take
a long time to make a breach. But though the walls were of
stone, the upper supports and the roof and most of the interior
were of wood, and some genius, directing the arrows of the Tartar
bowmen, gave them the order to concentrate upon the roof itself.

Each arrow, bearing at its tip a small bit of combustible substance like tar, soared up into the air like a tiny star, beautiful in
its flight could one but separate the idea of destruction from its
mission, and fell head first, penetrating the new boards as yet not
covered with metal or tile, and spreading a little blaze about.
One, two, three, the little fires grew—soon there were a dozen,
then a score, then it seemed as if a myriad of lights were twinkling.
A little wind sprang up at this minute, unluckily, and swept across
the Cathedral roof, fanning the points of light into a blaze. These
points grew greater, they united here and there one with another,
and then suddenly in leaps and bounds rushed together and the
flames embraced, and in a short time the whole Cathedral was in
the grip of a great conflagration.

Michael gazed up in alarm. There could be no safety now.
And through the church doors came the Greeks retreating, Kantakuzene at their head. They had barred the doors behind so that
the foe might be kept out until the flames made pursuit impossible,
and they joined with the boyars in the defence of the court in
front.

# THE STORMING OF KRYLOS

The enemy now were pressing on to certain victory. The blazing Cathedral could presage but one thing and that was the quick surrender of the Duke and his men. The Tartars threw themselves at the gates, a thousand beat upon them—the crowd surged—and then with great crashing and splintering the doors were down. Ahead of them lay victory and spoils. They rushed in to gain the booty before the flames had robbed them of the prey.

And then—it seemed as if the Heavens opened and played iron and flame down upon them.

"Open up on the west," shouted the astrologer across to the dwarf in the second tower.

The dwarf thrust his torch against three tubes. A short fuse burned and then the Heavens roared.

"The iron tubes—the iron tubes," exclaimed Michael below, seizing the girl's arm. "See, they are belching forth metal."

And in the iron hail which fell upon the attackers one could hear sudden shrieks and groanings and uproar where a moment before there had been shouts of triumph. Down went horse and rider, bowman and foot-soldier in that terrible hail.

"Open again," shouted Phokas, and again the tubes belched forth a deadly crop of iron and stone, and again Tartar horse and Tartar men went reeling down the slope, and in confusion into the meadows.

"Charge," shouted Lev, leaping with his men across the ruins of the Cathedral gate, and charge they did, driving the inner line of Tartars back through the old gate clear to the river's edge.

And now over their heads were still flying the iron and stones from the tubes in the tower. Caught unawares, and absolutely astounded, the Tartars were thrown into a panic; from some unknown hand, amidst the flashing and roar of they knew not what, they saw their own companions suddenly robbed of life or limb. These were the weapons with which devils fought.

"Back—back—" they cried, and the surging back of the van drove back the central body. And thrown into surprise by the charge of the Greeks and the boyars, they retreated from left and right as well as in the center, leaving the field of battle wholly to the defenders.

The Cathedral was a mass of flames now, its glare lighting up the whole Halich plain and throwing shadows even as far as the silvery Dniester and the blonie by its banks.

Kantakuzene had not rushed forward with the attack. Neither had Michael nor the old man. They stood by the foot of the towers watching the rout of the Tartars through the fallen gates.

"That is all. That is all. Now we must escape!" The shout came from Phokas, who with the dwarf came tumbling out of the entrances to the towers. "We have fired them all. The Tartars have abandoned the side roads and if we hurry then we can reach the river."

He led the way to the space in front of the towers and beckoned to Kantakuzene. The dwarf followed, and he who had once been emperor of the Eastern Roman Empire stepped out into the glare of the burning Cathedral, and then followed Phokas. They passed the place of the fallen gate and turned to the left. At this point the road dipped and they turned sharply to the right, to gain in a few steps the road to the ships over which Michael had been taken the night before. Those Greeks who had not gone with the Halich boyars followed the three; these in turn called to those far below, and soon all the Greeks, and the Bulgarians with them, were on the way to the ships. One who had been on guard hastened after the attacking party and told them of the chance to escape. They returned, Greeks, boyars, and Lev himself, and in a short time the Greek soldiery and the boyars were on the way to the galleys, while the Tartars still at a distance were drawing up their men, and the leaders were going about among them trying to preserve order. In the light of the burning church one could see as plainly as by day, though the retreat to the galleys was protected by the sloping hill and its shadow, and just beyond the shadow was the black forest, where none could see or pursue.

But it had come upon Michael, even in the midst of all this confusion, that that which meant escape to the others would probably only be the beginning of a new captivity for him; it flashed in his head, clearly, as the last Greek soldier disappeared over the slope, leaving behind in the court, now unbearably hot, only himself, the Duke, his daughter, and the old man and the dog. Even the boyars had followed the rest, without thought of their leader.

"And so it is," the boy pondered; "not one has sought safety for Duke Lev, or Katerina, whom they all were ready to worship scarce three hours ago. It is each for himself, truly. . . . And now I wonder what the Duke will do?"

They retreated from the court, for the Cathedral was now blazing throughout, and the heat was increasing, and beams and bricks were falling about them. It could be seen that of the Cathedral nothing would be left now, save perhaps some fragment of wall, for the falling roof and the blazing beams were bringing down the heavier masonry, cracked and blackened in the flames. What a sight it must be from below, the boy thought: the destruction had not been so magnificent when the Tartars under Batu-Khan first destroyed Halich. For even the Cathedral, that which they had spared, the most impressive building of all the ancient city—that building was now rising in fire. One could see it from the river for miles; a watcher on some Carpathian peak far away must have seen the blaze as it leaped into the air, the tongue of fire twisting and hissing and sputtering with the madness of a thousand dragons.

Farther and farther from the walls they retreated: then suddenly the Duke, as one coming from a trance, exclaimed: "See, the Greeks and my boyars are in retreat. Go after them, Katerina, and you, Michael, and you, old man, whom I know not."

He kissed his child and turned away from her resolutely.

"And will you not go?" she asked.

"I will remain," he said. "My plans are at an end. My dukedom exists no more. I am deserted even by my own men. That one whom men called Emperor has left me without a word. All that I had depended upon is now lost. Go—I will remain here to await the final issue."

But the child would not release him from her embrace. "Father, you must come." She sobbed, and clung to him.

"No, child," he released her arms by force, "and hurry, for now the last have gone over the hill. You show her the way," he commanded Michael. "Take her to safety."

But still she would not go, and the time was speeding on and the Tartars were massing their forces again, and even approached a little, cautiously, yet with few signs of panic left. "Go," he said, pushing her away from him sharply.

Michael took her and beckoning to the old man led the way to the slope, but even as he approached it, he saw that it would be no easy matter; the last of the fugitives had already passed into the woods—they were running at full speed, and an approaching band of Tartars were coming up the old road on their horses.

"By the lightning," he exclaimed, "we are too late."

As it proved finally, the bombardment of the Tartars, delivered by Phokas and the dwarf, had given barely time enough to save the whole party; the very last ones were indeed cut off by the Tartar riders who came back quickly after the first flight and repulse. And for the others who loitered those few fatal minutes upon the ground in front of the Cathedral, there was no hope at all.

They dashed back to the Duke who stood watching them with desperation written upon his features. "For us there is nothing but death," he exclaimed, "worse than death perhaps. But when it comes to certain capture, we will die rather than that." And he flourished his sword in the air, and beckoned to the others to arm themselves. Michael took two swords from fallen Tartars and gave one to the minstrel.

"They are coming," said the Duke.

And sure enough, the whole Tartar force was moving forward toward the Cathedral, and between them and that blazing pile stood only four figures, figures which stood out dramatically against that sea of flames: a boy, Michael; a golden-haired girl; an old man whose shadow loomed toward them gigantic and weird —and Duke Lev, the last of the family of Danilo, the son of Roman—the last of the Halich boyars.

# CHAPTER XV

## THE RESCUE

IT seemed to Michael as if the whole world were in motion before him. So splendid was the sight that he almost forgot the terror of it—the advancing horses, the upturned faces, the shining armor, and the glint of silver and gold. Across the whole plain the army was advancing, and brighter and brighter they stood in relief, as the flames roared higher and higher from the burning Cathedral. And not only were they coming closer, more and more rapidly, but the little company on the height came advancing down to meet them, driven by the terrific heat of the flames.

And now there was just an interval, before the first of the Tartar cavalry should be upon them. "Will they ride us down, or take us captive?" he questioned, and turning to Katerina grasped her hand. She was holding her father with one arm— on the farther side of Lev stood the Minstrel, his arm upon the Duke's shoulder—like a piece of statuary the four stood. The shouting increased; it grew to a roar—and then suddenly fell to a strange and overwhelming silence.

Michael looked up quickly; the Duke was shading his eyes so that he might see—the Minstrel was leaning forward—Katerina squeezed his hand suddenly; something had happened, something momentous, something well out of the ordinary.

For the moment it was a mystery, but the front line of the Tartars had come to a halt—yes, they were turning about to look in the opposite direction. They were upon a slightly rising ground and could look back over the men following. There was a cry, a command—the horses swept about and dashed off circling the nearest foot soldiers. And at the very instant when the four on Krylos expected to be ridden down, trampled, lassoed perhaps and driven away—the whole Tartar force was brought to a halt.

"What then means this?" demanded the Duke. "I can see nothing. Yet the whole army has ceased to move."

"There is something happening at the rear," said Katerina, her quick eyes catching the sudden resumption of action on the part of the distant rear guard—"they are swinging about."

Hope broke in upon Lev. "Perhaps the villagers are giving them stubborn battle and may divert them."

Then suddenly a sound like thunder broke upon the air.

"The Lechs," shrieked the Minstrel, "they are crossing the bridge. No other knights ride like that."

"It is," exclaimed Michael. "It is the Poles. They have come at last. Katerina—Katerina—" his triumphant eyes danced—"we are saved. Saved."

"Poles?" Duke Lev turned to the boy.

"Yes. I sent Stasko for them. My father must be there."

"You sent Stasko for them? When?"

"Two days ago. They must have ridden like the wind from Lvov. They are the King's own men, I have no doubt."

They could begin to see then the forms of great horsemen riding down upon the Tartars from the rear. But instead of fleeing up the slope of Krylos and thereby putting themselves in a trap, the Tartars were falling back into the plain along the foot of the hills that bordered the old city. Back—back—back—they went, swarming past the onlookers, who now instead of being in the battle were far to one side of it. In the front of the Tartar forces the horsemen were forming to charge the Poles, but the attack had come with such suddenness and with such force that there was little time left for the Tartars to re-form. However, they turned about and fought fiercely, as Tartars always fought, giving no quarter and expecting none, but thus far they dealt only with the advance guard of the Poles. The main body was crossing the smaller bridge of the Lukiev in ranks of four each. And lucky it was for the four on Krylos that the villagers had held the town and bridges firm, for otherwise the Poles must have taken to the water or have had recourse to the Bloody Ford by the blonie. And such fording might have had disastrous results, for the swollen river could have swept some of them away and broken the ranks of the cavalry. As it was, they had the bridge to cross by, and dashing through the cheering village they had sped over the smaller bridge of the Lukiev river and thrown themselves upon the rear of the advancing Tartars, almost before these had known that there was any trouble to be expected from the rear.

The lines deployed—formed anew—commands were given, and the Polish cavalry charged.

And such a charge!

There were a few thousand Tartars, spread out over the plain in such fashion that there seemed to be many more, and there were perhaps one quarter as many Polish horsemen. The horsemen wore light chain armor, with a reinforcement of plate across the chest; the helmets were light, the swords long and broad in order to strike better from the saddle. The horses were already steaming when they dashed across the bridge into Halich. They had come like the wind from Bolshov where they had been gathered together from separate squadrons sent out from Lvov. Among them were knights from Krakow and Poznan, szlachta from the country and towns, and gentry soldiers of various ranks from Lvov, Mazovia, and Silesia. But they all did the bidding of this new king, Kazimir—he who had united all the provinces into a solid kingdom—and they bore on their spears not the pennons of separate dukedoms but the white eagle on the red field.

*Charge.* The flashing of spears and the glint of swords. *Charge.* The lowered pennon with its point in among the ranks of the enemy. At first they rode close together, then gradually spreading as the enemy scattered, they covered the field like a flock of gigantic birds with gay feathers. What thoughts went through their minds might not be recalled by them nor related to others later; there was but one call. *Charge.* The flames from the burning Cathedral were rising high in the air lighting up the ghastly scene, the roofs of peasant houses all about them were shooting up in flames, huge shadows stalked up and down the plain as the smoke rolled up in gusts; this was destruction, this was the fruit of man's ambition upon earth. This was war. And all about them rose the cries of the wounded and the homeless, despoiled of all they owned. The cries of the Tartars, and the despairing shouts of the leaders attempting to gather the men for one last stand, mingled with the roar of the flames and the tumult of battle.

On they charged. It was the West against the East. And the East was scattered before the onrushing tide. On came the horsemen with the sweat like foam upon their horses' flanks; on they came like clouds driven through the sky by a great wind, irresistible, not to be denied. And in and among them rose into the air a clamor, the clash of metal, and the beating of hoofs upon the stones. There was in it all a vast melody, a song that beat with regular cadence through men's thoughts. *Charge.* Here stands a group to do battle, with barricades rolled hurriedly in the way, overturned carts, piles of lumber, trees. *Charge.* The crash of the advancing riders, the flashing of swords, the cries for mercy, and then on again to the next point where the enemy have made another hurried stand. The horsemen have gathered the impetus of comets rushing through space, nothing can stand before them, they ride, and ride, and ride. Though all the barricades of the world stood tonight before these madly riding troops nothing could stop them.

To right and left the Tartars flew. Some sought the Tchev river by a road through the hills and escaped to the farther bank. Some fled straight ahead past the lines of the old city walls and escaped to the south. Those who turned to the Lukiev and floundered in its lowlands were easily rounded up and made captives. One huge band that offered resistance just below the city walls in the Podgrodzie fought until the last man was killed. And when the cavalry had dispersed every unit and had made the living Tartars prisoners, and only a few fleeing men could be seen in the distance, then the leader turned across the bridge below Krylos and came up the road to the place where Duke Lev stood.

And as Duke Lev saw him and those who came after him, he went forward alone with his sword raised high, but he grasped the blade and not the hilt. "I surrender," he cried. "I surrender to the King of Poland." But the man on the horse did not accept the sword. Instead he looked at the other and bowed from the hips.

"Are you Duke Lev?" he asked.

"I am."

The rider drew from his garments a scroll weighted down with blood-red seals. "I have here," he said, "a pardon from our King. For he knew in advance what would take place here tonight. Take this, and live—and with this, safe conduct to whatever place you wish."

Duke Lev bowed his head.

Then leading his horse, the knight advanced to the place where the others stood, and at sight of him Michael ran forward and threw his arms about his neck. "Father," he shouted, "did you have word from Stasko?"

"I did. We came as soon as we could get enough men. I have taken those who were on duty in Lvov, men from all parts of Poland, and I have sent a message to the King telling him what has taken place. But who are these others?"

"This," said Michael, "is a poet and minstrel—a Pole. This other," and he caught at the girl's hand to bring her nearer, "this is the Golden Star of Halich."

# CHAPTER XVI

## WHOM GOD HATH JOINED

I T is now the month of Czerwiec, or the Month of Scarlet—which men in the West call June, when the earth is emblazoned with its most beautiful colors, and chief among them the scarlet of bright flowers which glows amidst the setting of green. And over the city of Lvov rises the song of merriment and gaiety, for this is a holiday in honor of the young warrior who comes back from the lands of the steppe to take his bride in the old church of St. John. Through the old grod or city of the Russini clustered about the slope of the castle hill, and the new city founded by Kazimir, there is the sound of music and dance, even now early in the morning when the sun is rising red over the hills. This warrior is one who has so well distinguished himself that nobles of the court have ridden here from Krakow; King Kazimir, alas, has been dead these two years, for it is now 1372, and King Louis who rules both Poland and Hungary is more kindly disposed toward the latter than the former.

As it is a holiday the country folk have been pouring in all night, arriving by cart, on horseback, or on foot. The whole city is alive with color and the fragrance of flowers, the gates are decked with banners and blossoms, and there are many bands of musicians ready to follow after the wedding procession when the festivities begin. Here are the Tsigan folk, and Stasko at their head; here are the Wallachians come up through the Dniester valley; here are the Armenians in great numbers—the Russini, the Jewish folk and Germans who live in their own sections of the city. Every kind of garment is seen in the crowd, from the rags of beggars to the purple of magnates, and much of the cloth worn by the peasants in holiday attire is richly embroidered in red and yellow and silver.

As the sun rises higher the gates of the new city are thrown open, and one may see that the road leading from the new central square to the Brama Krakowska or Krakow gate is the gayest of all, for the route of the procession is through this gate to the old church of St. John outside the walls. The Cathedral itself is not yet in state for such ceremonies; it was one of the last public acts of King Kazimir to place the foundation stone of this Cathedral, but many years were to pass before it was completed. And the old church of St. John, tiny and homelike, was to see the ceremony performed.

All at once there comes a fanfare of trumpets—a company of men on white horses richly caparisoned comes through the Krakow gate. Behind them soldiers marching—soldiers in light armor who have been out on the frontiers, men hardened in battle and accustomed more to fray than to festival. Then a group of *szlachta* gorgeously clad, and with them the bridegroom himself upon a horse. "Vivat—vivat," comes from the crowd, and the beggars rush in close—clang—clang—clang—the money thrown into the air strikes upon the street stones and there is a scramble among the poor folk. And as the procession moves, girls march along the street ahead throwing flowers into the road, until the highway is one mass of white and scarlet petals.

Then through another street comes another procession. Again come the youths on white horses, sounding the summons on trumpets that gleam like gold; more horsemen, clad in the costumes of every nation upon earth; pennants wave in the breeze—and then comes the bride. She is dressed in white, with a crown of flowers

[ 203 ]

surmounting a richness of hair that shines in the morning sun like pure gold. She rides seated upon a platform with a high roof, a modification of the sedan chair of the Western nations, and four youths in rich livery carry the precious burden. Beside her upon a magnificent horse rides her father; in other palanquins are borne the bridesmaids and maids of honor, and following them come the escorts of the *szlachta*. Though the bride wears a veil, yet the people know her name for it rings upon the lips of thousands.

She enters the church with her father, and at once the choir breaks forth in song. Then from the farther side enters the bridegroom—the music fills the air, and the sweetness of flowers is everywhere, and outside the crowds have suddenly become stilled for they hear the voice of the priest as he begins the chant of the nuptial mass. At length the youth and the bride are kneeling, and they are bound together with the band which the priest blesses and slips over their arms; the rings are given, and the last chorus is sung, and the bridegroom has kissed the bride upon the lips.

They turn from the altar. O joyous day that begins a life with such great promise! And as they go from the church there approaches them an old minstrel who has just come in from the border, and from the musical instrument which he carries rises the song of the happy wedding of a prince and princess of old days. Bright shines the sun, and bright upon them fall the wishes of their friends and loved ones. And this is the end of the story of Michael Korzets and the Golden Star of Halich.

*The Wedding of the Golden Star*

(Church of St. John, Lvov, in background; ornaments and capitals from Armenian
Gospel of 1198; musical instruments from Municipal Museum in Lvov,
and studies of Matejko)

*Halich Today*

(Ornament from portal of St. Stanislaus; double
capitals from fragments found on Krylos Hill)

# Epilogue

# There Was a City

THERE was a city, the name of it Halich, yet where it
stood the sun today sweeps gloriously across fields of
wheat that sway and whiten in the wind, and from the
meadows comes the call of the boy driving in the cattle, or the
goose-girl assembling her flock.   It turns to gold the jagged rocks
up high there on that cliff where once men built castles to with-

stand Tartar and Turk, castles builded upon the ruins of older castles where the early Slavs perhaps held off Romans or Greeks. It flicks into diamonds the ripples of the almost-hidden Lukiev, the river which flows to the Dniester, dreaming of the days when it was once the Lukva, and past the wharves upon its banks rode the lading boats and small galleys from the Black Sea.

A boy comes singing up the road; a girl at the doorway of a humble cottage weaves some thousand-year-old pattern into the cloth where her needle darts in and out; a few black kruks or ravens sweep by; the peasant driving his oxen up the road and across the field stops to shake his whip over a spring to frighten the frogs, and in doing so dislodges a pebble that was once a part of some ducal throne, while from the spring glares up at him as if in reflection the carven face of some hero of old, a stone ornament that once graced a cornice.

What else is there here to tell that once upon this fertile land a great city reared its head? That along the hills and over the ridges, the domes and spires of Tserkievs and churches threw outlines into the sky? That here were busy streets and markets, and emperors and slaves may have stood upon this very spot where we now stand, contemplating a vast and populous city, marveling at the ingenuity of builders and the thrift of merchants? What is there to recall this departed glory? There are the stones of the road, there are cellars into which ploughshares sometimes descend when the peasants are turning earth; there is that stone polygon out in the field where red beets grow, where once stood a Cathedral altar; heroes' graves are out there amidst the corn, those yellow pumpkins are ripening along ruined castle walls. A war-marred doorway in yonder church tells of a departed day.

There is naught here save silence and sweet sounds, the softness of undefiled air. . . . Is it to this end that men struggle, build cities, create empires? Is it that in the end always come silence

# THERE WAS A CITY

and solitude and peace? The sun is setting across the western hills, the mists rise up from the river, and there comes to the heart, despite its sadness, the quiet content which perfect peace brings. And though in the mind's eye one sees those trains of humanity that have swept across the scene, the Goths, the Huns, the Rus, the Poles, the Hungarians, the Greeks, the Germans— millions of them since the beginning of time—peoples who have imposed their thoughts upon this land in creations of brick and wood and stone—yet one looks about in vain for a single sign of all their strivings. And yet those strivings were here at our feet! Shall all our hurryings upon earth be thus forgotten? Shall all our endeavors resolve themselves into this great peace and silence? Whatever the answer, there comes into our musing a sudden burst of happiness and joy, for these things are of the past and of the present. And all Eternity lies ahead.

# NOTES

Although many might regard it as a fantastic speculation, the idea of the *Third Rome* was prevalent among Slavic peoples for centuries. Indeed, in a recent number of the Slavonic Review (June, 1930) Jaroslav Bidlo mentions the matter in an article entitled *"The Slavs in Medieval History."* He discusses conditions after the fall of Constantinople in 1453, telling of the Slav refugees who fled to Russian lands and preached the necessity of freeing orthodox Christians from the rule of the Turks. The new Roman Empire was to be set up in Eastern Europe at this date, with Moscow as the Third Rome. Ivan Third (1462–1505) married a niece of the last Byzantine Emperor. Her name was Sophia Paleologa, and through her, Ivan considered himself the heir of the Byzantine Emperors, and the defender of Orthodox Christianity.

Before going to the site of the ancient city of Halich (Polish *Halicz*—Russian *Galitsch*) I was quite prepared after reading some thirty or forty sources on the history of the Red Land or Red Rus or *Czerwien,* to be able to locate the positions of the old buildings, the castles, the Cathedral, and the main churches. The principal work which had come my way was the volume, "Three Historical Treatises of the Principality of Halicz," *Trzy Opisy Historyczne Staroksiazecego Grodu Halicza,* published by Gubrynowicz i Schmidt, Lvov, 1883, in which a historical summary had been added to the description of the excavations carried on by the author, Dr. Izydor Szaraniewicz, and others.   At that time I believed that the Grod or Ducal Castle was located in the fields and heights south of the present church of St. Stanislaus, once St. Pantalemon.

But once in the actual country I found that the whole matter had been thoroughly investigated and determined by Dr. Alexander Czolowski, municipal director of the museums in Lvov, a scholar, historian and antiquary; he placed the location of the ancient Grod on Krylos, a tongue-shaped piece of land some four miles south of the present town of Halicz.   This location of the ducal Grod on Krylos is confirmed by a later work by Dr. Joseph Pelenski, a sumptuous publication under the name "Halicz," published by the Academy of Science in Krakow in 1914.   Upon visiting Krylos one sees immediately that, tradition aside, there could be no other point of vantage in Halicz so suitable to the purposes of a ducal castle.   The land, natural fortifications, position of streams and bridges, correspond almost identically to that ideal fortress of Viollet-Le-Duc in his book "Annals of a Fortress" in which he tells of the experience of the walled town, castle, medieval fortress, and modern fort of La Roche-Point on the French frontier.

Halicz preserves some of its charm in a few crumbling walls and ancient stone foundations with the Dniester sweeping about it like a half-moon, and the Lukiev and Tchev (now the Lomnica) draining lazily to the larger river; but from the castle where the Potockis and others held the frontiers of civilization one sees only farm lands and orchards.   It brings the thought that Poland has from the very beginning defended Central Europe from Eastern invasions all through this territory, and that descendants of the Lechs and Poles who were driven out of this country by Vladimir a thousand years ago came back after the extinction of the boyars to save the lands from absolute destruction at the hands of Asiatic peoples.   On every hand the ruins of castles and forti-

KRAKOW
PRZYMSL
SAMBOR · LVOV (LWOW)
POLAND
TREMBOVLA
Trail
KIEV
MUSCOVY
GRAND DUCHY of LITHUANIA
DNIEPER-GREEK BORYSTHENES
HALICH (HALICZ)
TO KIEV
KAMINETS
Road to Bude-Peth
CARPATHIANS
DNIESTER
GREEK TYRAS
Black Trail
HUMAN
DNIEPER
HUNGARY
MOLDAVIA
(Old Roman Road)
Wallachian Trail
BESARABIA
BIALOGROD (AKKERMAN)
KRYM (CRIMEA)
WALLACHIA
BLACK SEA
MAP OF
HALICH
IN 1362
DANUBE →
BULGARIA
By ship to
TSARGROD
(CONSTANTINOPLE)

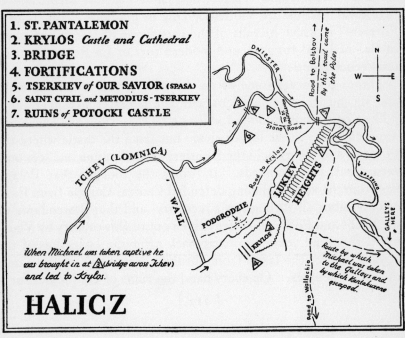

1. ST. PANTALEMON
2. KRYLOS *Castle and Cathedral*
3. BRIDGE
4. FORTIFICATIONS
5. TSERKIEV *of* OUR SAVIOR (SPASA)
6. SAINT CYRIL *and* METODIUS - TSERKIEV
7. RUINS *of* POTOCKI CASTLE

DNIESTER →
Road to Bolsbov
By this road came the Poles.
N
W — E
S
Stone Road
Road to Krylos
TCHEV (LOMNICA)
WALL
LUKIEV HEIGHTS
PODGRODZIE
KRYLOS
GALLEYS HERE
Road to Wallachia
Route by which Michael was taken to the Galleys and by which Kantakuzene escaped.

*When Michael was taken captive he was brought in at ③ (bridge across Tchev) and led to Krylos.*

HALICZ

fications rise into the air and in chapel vaults and mounds are piled high the bones of those Poles who defended this soil.

I wish to acknowledge my debts to authorities in Lvov who put at my disposal the exact material that I wanted. Dr. Czolowski took much time to acquaint me with the treasures of which Lvov is possessed—and reserved for me the books which dealt with this country in old days. His own History of Lvov was my guide in recreating the Lvov of 1362. I am under a great debt as well to Director Kazimir Tyszkowski of the Ossolinski Library, whose preparation of books on the subject of Halicz and Czerwien was so excellent that I was able to cover the known field in an incredibly short time.